Caroline H Woods

Woman in Prison

Caroline H Woods

Woman in Prison

ISBN/EAN: 9783744747219

Printed in Europe, USA, Canada, Australia, Japan

Cover: Foto ©Andreas Hilbeck / pixelio.de

More available books at **www.hansebooks.com**

WOMAN IN PRISON.

BY

CAROLINE H. WOODS.

NEW YORK:

PUBLISHED BY HURD AND HOUGHTON.

Cambridge: Riverside Press.

1869.

RIVERSIDE, CAMBRIDGE:
STEREOTYPED AND PRINTED BY
H. O. HOUGHTON AND COMPANY.

WHY WRITTEN.

———◆———

I WAS reading an evening paper. I glanced over the advertisements. One attracted my attention, and held it so strongly that I read it over and over, again and again. There was nothing unusual in it to ordinary observation. It read, " Wanted. — At the Penitentiary, a Matron. Inquire at the Institution."

I turned the paper over to read the general news; but could not place my thoughts so as to comprehend the meaning of the words before my sight. Without the intention to do so, I looked again at the advertisement. It became a study to me.

Said Thought — If you were to answer that advertisement, and obtain the situation, it would place you upon missionary ground, and at the same time give you employment which would afford you a support while you are teaching the ignorant. You would get knowledge in the position. A new phase of life would be opened to your view. You would have an opportunity to observe, practically, how well the present system of prison discipline is adapted to reform convicts, and repress crime. But the cost is too much. I cannot become a Matron in a Penitentiary.

I laid the paper down, without reading it, because I could see nothing in it except that advertisement.

The next day I went in town, sat down in the office of a friend, and took up a morning paper. No sooner had I opened it than that advertisement spread itself out before me. It changed the form of its appeal; left out what my selfishness might gain, to enlist my compassion and aid, entirely, in what I might accomplish for others. It called to me, in piteous tones, to go work for the prisoner. It was the echo of a voice that I long ago heard, Come into our prisons, and help us, we beseech you!

I cannot! I have other things to do, and they are as much for the benefit of humanity as anything I may be able to accomplish for you. My spirit darkened as I made the answer; a cloud of guilt settled down upon it. I threw down the paper in order to dissipate it, and to avoid the plea.

I turned and talked with my friend; but my thoughts were not in what we were saying. That advertisement followed them, and filled them to the exclusion of every other subject.

In the abstraction which it caused the hour in which I was to leave the city passed, and I missed my train. I must remain and avail myself of another.

While I was waiting, that advertisement returned to my reflections, and urged its cause imperatively as a command. It was a call, to me, resistless as the voice that awoke the young Israelitish Prophet from his slumbers. In another moment the struggle with my pride was over, and my spirit answered, — I will go, even to lust-besotted Sodom if thou leadest, Light of my path!

I seated myself in a street car, went to the prison, applied for the place, and obtained it.

Day by day I wrote down what I saw and heard, what I said and did. Why? In obedience to the same Voice that called me to the work.

The tale is before you.

May it touch the heart of every one who reads the story, and melt it into a compassion which will labor for the redemption of the prisoner; into a pity which will echo around the cry — Open the prison doors, not to let the prisoner go free, but to let in, to him, the light of moral knowledge, and the discipline of Christian charity.

CONTENTS.

I.

FIRST DAY IN PRISON.

It was Saturday morning that I became an inmate of the Penitentiary.

I was conducted to the kitchen, where I was to oversee the cooking for the prisoners, and to the prison adjoining it, which I was to see kept in order, by the Deputy Master of the institution, who gave me my keys and installed me in my office of Prison Matron.

When we first went in he called the six women who do the work in the kitchen, and the three "sweeps" who keep the prison clean, to him, and presented their new mistress, in my person, to them.

They were convicts that surrounded me at his call; but they were human beings. Human faces looked up to mine for sympathy and care. Some of them were fine looking, even in their coarse uniform, some were pretty as I picked them out one by one. They all looked at me earnestly, for a few moments, as though they were reading their sentence of harshness or kindly treatment, under my rule, in my face; then, turned away to their work again.

They whispered as they stood together, and I saw by their furtive glances that they were watching, and

1

discussing me, as I walked around to take a survey
of my new field of labor. They were undoubtedly
commenting upon my personal appearance; and
making their predictions as to my sharpness in detecting their impositions, and ability to control their
perverseness; or, I imagined so.

The Deputy showed me the mush boiler, that
would cook two large tubs full of that farinaceous
edible at a time; the potato steamer, that would
hold four barrels of that esculent vegetable at
a cooking; the soup and coffee kettles, of still
larger dimensions; and that comprised all of the apparatus required in preparing the mammoth meals
which were to serve above four hundred people.
These cooking utensils were kept in operation by
pipes conducting steam to them from a boiler stationed in the middle of the room.

When he put the steam boiler under my direction I shrank back in terror from the task of managing it. The huge culinary apparatus, which he
had been exhibiting, although outside the pale of
ordinary housekeeping, was still within the reach of
my understanding; but I had no idea of the management of steam; it was not only a difficult, but
dangerous affair.

"The house will surely be blown up if you leave
the care of that upon me," I said to him.

"You must watch it very closely."

"I don't know how, and I have no aptness for
learning that kind of science."

"One of the women will tend it." And he went on with explanations that were all Greek to me. "It is safe when you have on twenty pounds of steam. There is your gauge," and he pointed to a clock-like looking affair on the wall. "That hand will move round and tell you how much steam you have on. You must keep water enough in the boiler or you will get blown up. If it runs from that centre stopcock, on the side, it is safe. You notice that glass tube in front. The water is just as high in that as it is in the boiler. This faucet is to let the water off if you get the boiler too full. Turn that faucet when you let the water on," and he went along and pointed to one in a pipe by the wall, "and that pump is there in case of accident. You must have it worked every day so as to keep it in order."

All knowledge is useful, I thought, and in time I shall understand running a steam-engine. As the women have been trusted with the dangerous thing, they may still continue to be, till I have leisure to learn the science of steam as applied to cooking.

After I had taken a survey of the kitchen the Deputy took me into the women's prison which led out of it.

The centre of the hollow square, in which the dormitories are built, looked like a huge block of glittering ice, so white were the washed walls of brick and stone. The black, grated doors of the cells, inserted into them, like the teeth of grinning demons, were ranged along the sides about two feet apart, tier after tier, five stories, one above another.

The Deputy led me along past the iron **doors.** I trembled and shrank back; **but I** had no idea **of** receding from my **undertaking.** I " screwed my courage to the sticking-point," and looked **into the** narrow, stone rooms; but it was many days before **I** could force **myself to enter one.**

I grew heart-sick, and faint with **apprehension of** unknown terrors at their cheerless aspect.

" What lodgings for human beings ! " **I exclaimed.**

" They are not very pleasant," said the Deputy.

" **If you** were the one to blame **for it I** should certainly charge you with great inhumanity."

" **I** suppose you **will** think **us very cruel** sometimes."

" **In** this case **I** don't **know as you can help it. You did** not make these sleeping apartments for the **prisoners.** The **public** functionaries of the State **may be** thanked for showing such tender mercies as these."

" We are used to seeing them, and they **don't look** to us as they do to **you."**

" Does that make them any more comfortable for the prisoners ? Do **they get** used to them so as to be comfortable ? "

" I presume **so.** I know they are more comfortable places than some **had** before they came here."

" Then it should be the work **of the** vaunting Christianity of this religious land to raise such degradation to cleanliness, comfort, and respectability."

" There might be a **great** deal done in that direction if people were only disposed to do it."

" Our prisons are rather private affairs, I believe. They can only be visited on certain days and occasions."

" **It would be very** inconvenient for **our work to** have people **running in, and** over the place **at all times. We** could **not have it. And it** wouldn't be liked by the prisoners to be gazed at constantly."

I made no reply ; but I thought it might have a salutary effect **upon the** discipline of the prison. which he had just said I might think cruel, **to** be exposed to the **observation of** the **public. The** prisoners must have lost the sensibility which would shrink from being made **a spectacle before they came in** there. If visiting **were allowed only on** certain days and occasions, **the** place and the convicts would **be** put in order for company, and a very incorrect idea of the every-day life of the prisoners would **be o**btained.

If there were liberty to visit the **place, every** day, **many might go from curiosity, and it might** become annoying. **That very** curiosity might discover **and** discuss faults **in the** management, which **ought to** be remedied, and thus produce a counterbalancing benefit.

The officers might dislike such scrutiny, especially, if they were not doing their duty. They are officers of the government. Is it not proper that their conduct should be looked after by **the people** as much as that of any other government official ?

Evil comrades might go in and **hold** improper communication with the prisoners. Can they **not** do that on regular visiting days ?

Is it not only the work of humanity to see that crime is punished in a way that will not increase it; but also that of the legislator as a matter of civil policy; and that of the taxpayer as a matter of personal interest. It should interest every man and woman as a matter of personal protection from the depredations of vice to know how convicts are treated, and to judge whether that treatment tends to reform the criminal, or to harden and lead him deeper into crime when he is let out into the world again to pursue his own ways.

Ought the punishment of criminals, who have been tried, convicted, and sentenced publicly, to be conducted in secret? It is to be presumed that the keeper of the prison is trusty. There should be no presumption in the matter. It should be known that he is so, and he should be kept so by the ceaseless vigilance of public inspection. What is the quarterly, or semi-annual visit of fifty or a hundred men when the visit has been notified, and the prison put in order for their reception, towards effecting that?

My residence in that prison led me to see that the descriptions of Dickens, and his compeers in the regions of fictitious writing, have given, not the poetic illusions of imaginary sufferings to the contemplation of the world — hardly a vivid picture of the truth.

God speed the day when our prisons and penitentiaries may take a place beside public schools, orphan asylums, houses of refuge, all institutions for the cultivation of a knowledge which tends to the elevation of virtue, and the suppression of vice, in the care of the public !

Our own children may not stimulate to an interest in them. Our own children may not require the benefit of the public school, or orphan asylum; but somebody's children will. In working for the elevation of everybody's children are we not benefiting our own ?

After he had shown me around, so that I might take a general survey of my field of labor, the Deputy left me with my charge, saying, —

" You are mistress here. No one has a right to interfere with you, and you are responsible to no one but me, or the Master."

" But the Head Matron will, of course, come and instruct me in the details of my work. I must know what work belongs to each woman, and how she is expected to perform it."

" The women know their work and will do it. The most you have to do is to keep order."

" That may be a man's idea of managing a kitchen ; but there are a great many details that I ought to understand in order to get the work properly done, and done in its proper time ; and with the greatest ease to myself and the women."

" The other Matrons will tell you. I will tell you all I can."

I thought, but I did not say it, — You are better disposed than informed. He saw by the anxious expression of my face that I was not satisfied, and added, " The women know, they will tell you."

I made no reply; but I thought — It is not the proper thing for me to receive my instructions from the convicts. It is their place to be instructed by me. If I am taught by them, I am placed in an inferior position to them. In order to entertain a proper respect for me they should look up to me as their superior in all things.

The arrangement for receiving my directions from them placed me too much in their power also. It would be only indulging natural proclivities to "play off" on me under the circumstances; and I could hardly expect these poor, abandoned creatures to be superior to the temptation to do it when the opportunity was afforded them.

I could not consider such teachers reliable. If, by misleading me, with regard to a rule of the institution, they could obtain an indulgence, or relieve themselves of a burden, would they not take the advantage which they had of me and do it. I was suspicious that they would.

There was, probably, some pride mixed with these considerations, that rebelled against becoming a pupil of convicts when I was their mistress.

I stood looking on, or walking around, watching the movements of the women very narrowly, till one of the other Matrons came in. Then, I went to her with a volume of questions.

To most of them I received the answer, —

"I don't know about that particularly. I have never had anything to do with this department."

"Then, how am I to learn my duties, and get definite orders for the regulation of my work? Is there no Head Matron, no superior officer in the women's prison to whom I can go?"

"The Master's wife is enrolled as Head Matron, and receives pay as such, but she never comes round."

"I would go to her if I knew where to find her."

"I don't think she knows much more about it than you do, if you were to go to her. We will all tell you."

"But you don't know. If there is a Head Matron, and she is paid for doing the duties of one, why does she not perform them? Is she enrolled head offi-cer of this prison merely to obtain the salary? The government is very obliging to make her office a sinecure."

I was already perplexed — I was beginning to get vexed.

"Her husband does them for her, perhaps."

"Perhaps! Then why is he not here, to tell me the work which belongs to each woman, and how she is to do it; what work is required, and how I am to get my things to do with? But how can the Master attend to his own duties and those of the Head Matron too?"

"The Deputy will tell you."

"He must have his own duties to attend to — how can he perform hers? He is just as willing to tell me as you are, and I don't think he knows any more about my place than you do."

" The women know, they will tell you."

I was thrown back upon the convicts again for my instructions.

I went on, despairing of help, to study them out as best I could. Sometimes by asking left-hand questions of the women, and sometimes by getting direct explanations from them; but chiefly by watching the progress of the work. The place seemed to me full of disorder, confusion, and dirt.

When the Deputy came round again, I was full of trouble.

He said, when I complained to him, —

" You will find things in confusion. The Matron who went away yesterday was inefficient."

" Perhaps so," I replied; " but the confusion appears to me to date farther back than the last Matron. It arises from the want of a head officer to regulate affairs."

" I have double the trouble on this side, with four Matrons and a hundred women, than with three hundred men and more than a dozen officers on the other."

" You would insinuate that women are more difficult to get on with than men. I make a very different solution of the difficulty in this particular case. You are on the ground all of the time; explain his duty to every officer, and see that he does it. That makes the officer's work distinct before him. It is done under your eye, which makes it promptly and well done. If that were the case on this side, we might be as orderly, and have as little trouble in performing our part, as you on yours. The cook tells me that certain work belongs to the slide woman; the slide woman says it belongs to the sink women; the sink women shift it on the steam woman, and so I am kept on the chase, from one to another, for some one to do a piece of labor. I do not know who ought to do it, and they know it. If they do not intend to confuse me, they intend to clear themselves of all the work they can."

" Use your own judgment, and call on whom you please. They are all obliged to obey any order that you give."

" If I call upon one to do the work that has formerly been done by another, I stir up ill feelings among the prisoners towards each other, and contention, and they think me hard and unjust. It makes me trouble. They obey my order reluctantly, and say, ' That isn't my work.' "

" If they quarrel, they know the punishment. If they refuse to obey your orders, report them to me. and I will put them where they will be glad to obey." He nodded towards the prison door.

I knew he must refer to some kind of punishment. I did not know what; but frightful visions of the cruelties of which I had read rose in my imagination, and I said no more.

I vowed to myself that I would never get them punished by refusing to obey my unjust exactions if I could help it.

My thoughts did not stop with my words. I reasoned with myself. If my ignorance, or bad management, cause me to be unjust towards those women, and if I, by my injustice, arouse their bad temper so as to cause them to be punished, who will be most in fault? I decided that I should be. The question suggested itself to me — If you get them punished unjustly who will avenge them? The All-seeing-Eye will notice, and avenge it. I will be careful.

I resolved to feel my way along softly and carefully. There was no relief for my dilemma, except in my own ingenuity to find out the ways of the place, and the proper management to apply to it.

AT NIGHT.

At seven o'clock, P. M., came the marching in to supper, and the locking up of all the prisoners.

I looked to see, as they filed past me, one by one, if they carried marks of their crimes upon their faces. I saw nothing unusual in the mass; occasionally an individual countenance betrayed the vicious habits which had brought the woman there. If I had not known that they were convicts, I should never have suspected them to be different from the ordinary poor people who are constantly passing along the streets.

About sixty of the women in the Penitentiary were employed in the shop upon contract vests, pantaloons, coats, and shirts. There were about fifty employed upon sewing-machines. The rest cut, basted, and finished the work.

There were from four to ten in the wash-room. These were all lodged in my domain, with the exception of two or three who slept in the hospital.

When they left their work, at night, they were placed in file, in the order of their cells, and marched into the prison past the ration door, where their meals were handed out to them, through a slide, from the kitchen.

Their supper was a " skillet pan " of mush, or a slice of bread, and a quart of rye coffee, which was taken to their cells to be eaten after they were locked in their rooms — or stone dens, I called them in my indignation. The sight of those little, cramped stone cells recalled to my memory the pictures of dungeons, and imprisonments, and tortures which I had looked at in my childhood till my heart was racked with agony at the cruelties which they portrayed.

It was no paper picture that I was looking upon, but a stern reality; and my shrinking spirit asked again and again, as I saw those poor creatures marched in, and immured for the night, — Why did your folly prompt you to undertake such work?

Never shall I forget the hissing creak of the sliding bar as it closed them in ; or the click of the lock as I turned the key in it, for the first time, upon those poor wretches. Long before I got through with the thirty-six locks, it fell to my share to bolt, my fingers were bruised, and my arm ached ; but not so much as my heart.

I looked in upon the poor things, one by one, as I locked them in. An agony of pity worked itself into my soul, and oppressed me almost to suffocation.

I said to myself — Is this a woman's work ? May be. If it must be done, it should be done tenderly. Great God, for Christ's sake, pity them in their cold, damp, narrow cells, and make their straw pallets couches of rest! I prayed mentally as I left the grated doors.

I had thought this to be missionary ground. I might teach some of them the way to Eternal Life, and the way to reformation. Alas! I found little chance with those who went to the shop and wash-room. They rose at sunrise, and worked till sunset. No one was allowed to hold communication with them, but their own Overseer, about their work. Neither were they allowed to talk in their cells at night, and they would have been too tired if they had been given the liberty to do so. The task-master had been over them all day to drive them, pitilessly, to fulfill their sentence of so many months hard labor in the Penitentiary.

I turned away, sadly, from that disappointed hope; but I saw the opportunity still before me to teach the nine, whom I had under my immediate care, to gov-ern their tempers, and their passions, and to lead a new life. It was teaching only that could effect it. They were ignorant of the way to do it.

My bonnet and shawl had lain all day upon the table that was placed for my use in the kitchen. The woman, who was to wait upon me in my room, had asked if she should take them up. I had said, no, thinking I might find time to go with her; but that opportunity did not offer.

After the women were locked up, the Receiving Matron said to her, "Take those things to our room! We will go up now," she said to me.

I started back as she led me to the stone stairs of the prison, and began to ascend them.

" Where are we going ? " I asked in surprise.

" Our room is up here," she replied quietly.

" In the prison ! are we to sleep in the prison ? "

" Yes."

She made no further comment. It was too late in the day to recede or demur. I followed her up, up, up, over five stone flights, along a stone walk to the farther end of the building, through a grated door, into a room made up of a half dozen cells with a dormer window in the roof. Some straw had been thrown down upon the stone floor, and an old woolen carpet laid over it. The walls were of stone like the cells, and whitewashed like them. There were some wooden chairs, an old bureau, two sinks, and two single beds, arranged on opposite sides of the room. In one corner was a double wardrobe, apparently to be shared in common by both Matrons.

I had not given my own accommodations a thought in taking my place in the prison. In all institutions of the kind which I had ever been in, each Matron had a nice bedroom to herself, in a comfortable part of the house, and most of them comfortable sitting-rooms attached. It never occurred to me that a female officer, in any public institution, could be requested to occupy such a room. However I could bring myself to it for the sake of carrying out the purpose that induced me to take the place.

I stood a moment, and looked all round the room.

I then examined the bed. It was clean, and looked comfortable.

" Is this all the room, and are these all the comforts we are to have?" I asked of the Receiving Matron.

" You see all," she replied. "If we had more, we should have no time to enjoy them."

" Rather a sorry prospect if one is to take herself into consideration at all. Is there a bath-room that we can use? To take a bath would be really refreshing, and help me to sleep to-night, I am so tired."

" I am tired all of the time, and there is no chance to rest. We must rise at four in the morning, and be on the spring every moment till eight in the evening; you will be on duty till nine, because you receive the keys at that hour."

" Every day?"

" Every day!"

" There is usually a Relief Matron in such institutions, so that the other Matrons can have rest."

" There used to be one here; but, instead of that, there is an Assistant Matron in the shop."

" Then the Shop Matron has all of the relief, and the others none. Why is that?"

" They want to get as much work done in the shop as possible, to support the institution, the Master says. When I get tired, and feel like grumbling, I tell them it is money taken out of our flesh and blood to make the institution rich."

"It is probably the way the Master takes to recommend himself to the Board of Directors. They like him for his thrift in managing."

"I don't know where the money goes; but I know we are worked to death. I am dying by inches."

"Why must I be up an hour later than the rest to receive the keys?"

"Because you have them in charge during the night, those that stay in the prison. If you are out, I take them."

"Out! What time have I to go out?"

"Three evenings in the week, after the prisoners are locked up, if you wish."

"What time have I then?"

"You can be gone till four o'clock in the morning, if you like."

"When shall I sleep?"

"You can make your own arrangements for that. Perhaps on the way, if you take a horse car."

"I am afraid to go out evenings alone; but in that relief I can get a bath."

"I forgot your question about the bath-room. There is none, that I know of, for the officers' use. There is one in the house for the Master's family. I don't know whether the Matrons that lodge there are allowed to use it."

"Then some of the Matrons are lodged comfortably in the house. Why is that distinction made?"

"I don't know. There are bathing-tubs, for the prisoners, in my wash-house. I never use them; but if you wish to, you can. They are scrubbed out clean."

" I must be up from four A. M., 'till nine P. M. That makes seventeen hours of labor."

" Sometimes you will be required to sit up one, two, or three hours later."

" Why ? "

" The Master's wife or daughters may have company, and keep the women up-stairs. We have to sit up and wait for them to come in, so as to lock them up."

" And be up all the same at four next morning ? "

" Yes."

" Do the Master's wife and daughters get up at four the next morning, after sitting up so late, and go to work ? "

" Of course not."

" If the wife is Head Matron, has she not her duties to do in the morning as well as we? And ought she not to see that the other officers are not worked like that? If she possesses the common feelings of humanity, she would provide some relief, if it were in her power."

" There is not much humanity in exercise here. We are all too hard worked to think of any one but ourselves."

" I should think that might be your case."

" I often tell them it is as much a House of Correction for the officers as the prisoners."

" Ten hours of labor is now considered a good

day's work. To drag the convicts from sunrise to
sunset only exhausts them. They do not get through
with as much work as they would do in ten hours,
and the intervening time given to rest."

"That has been an established rule here for fifty
years or more."

"It is certainly a very antiquated idea, all of a
half century old. I recollect hearing my grandfather
say that people worked that way when he was a boy.
But people's ideas have changed since that time, and
the people of this generation consider such demands
of labor very unreasonable."

"The only changes here have been to make things
harder. They will put upon you all they can make
you do."

If she had been telling the truth that was a plain,
but correct statement of facts.

"How long has the present Master had charge
here?"

"Forty-five or fifty years."

"It is no wonder that his heart has become like the
nether millstone. No man ought to remain in such a
place such a length of time. The best human heart
that ever beat would become ossified, if it ever entertained human feelings, if compelled to exercise such
continued tyrannous exactions."

"I don't know whether he ever had human feelings — he does not exercise much humanity, as I
regard it, now."

"But he does not make the laws for the regulation

of the institution. There must be State laws and a Board of Overseers to which he is accountable. There must be printed regulations for the management of this prison. I will get them from the Deputy to-morrow."

"If you can, you will accomplish more than the rest of us have been able to do."

"I can try."

"You can try, and I hope you will succeed. The rest of us have been told that there were no printed rules that would do us any good. It may be a benefit to the rest of us if you succeed."

I lay down upon my bed. Sleep was out of the question. The effluvia of a hundred human bodies came up through our open door, rank with nauseous odor. I got up and opened our one window to its utmost extent, first asking my room-mate if it would be disagreeable to her to have it left so.

Fatigue even would not overcome the noise of the rattling buckets, the snoring, coughing, and groaning of the tired women. If I closed my eyes, my head was in confusion. I was going up, up, up over the stone steps, and looking over the rails down the dizzy height, to the stone floor below.

I lay thinking over my prison prospects. Seventeen hours of regular labor, to which might be added occasionally, one, two, or three more. The other seven, with the noise of that prison ringing in my ears, and the care of it, if accident or sickness intervene. How long can any constitution bear such a strain? Surely the **Board of Directors** cannot understand how things are managed here. They cannot understand the amount of work which is demanded by the Master of his female Prison Matron. One other was no more favored, by her own account.

I was glad when the four o'clock bell rung me up to my duties.

III.

SECOND DAY IN PRISON.

THERE was a small bell hung directly over my head; the wire from it reached into the men's prison. It was rung by the watchman at four o'clock in the morning, to call me up.

I sprang out of bed at the first tinkle, threw a shawl around me, put my feet into my slippers, ran down, unlocked my steam woman to make her fire, and my cook to start her breakfast. I let them into the kitchen, and locked them in. Then, I went back to dress myself.

Up, up, over the five flights, past the grated doors, over the stone walks. The air of that prison sent a chill over me like that of a tomb. Were not those cells the tomb of love, of hope, of peace, and respectability! In them lay buried all of this world's success, all that it values: how much of the inheritance of the life to come God knows. Those black doors were a pall of disgrace of deeper dye than that which covers the coffin with its lifeless clay. I was chilled through and through by my thoughts and the objects that engendered them. And those objects were to be ever there before my sight, while I remained in prison, and those thoughts must ever arise to be my company. I could escape; no prison bar was slid upon me to keep me there; but the convicts *must* remain. The unyielding lock, the unremitting toil, the pursuing regret, and the torture of remorse were before them, upon them, within them.

I might be able to speak to them a word of pity, of hope in a better life to come. The thought gave me courage to go to my day's work.

I took no unnecessary time for personal adorning; but my fingers were benumbed and moved slowly. I had scarcely finished dressing when the "first bell" rung.

That was the large bell in the yard that called all of the prisoners from their beds.

At that signal I was to assist in unlocking the rest of the women. If they were not out of their beds when the key was put in the lock, they were called to sharply by the Matron who was with me —

"Come, get up! How dare you lie there after the first bell has rung!"

It might prove necessary to talk to some laggards in that harsh way; but I would try some other method, with those of whom I had the care, first.

Yawning, and groaning, and moaning, they dragged themselves out of their beds and made them up. After this was done they tied them up against the wall with a cord which was attached to the iron bars upon which the bed rested, and then passed over a hook in the side of the cell. Then, they stood waiting for the second bell, which was the signal for them to go to work.

Poor, pitiable objects, they looked, as they were mustered for the long day's drill of thankless, unrequited toil. They worked without a motive, and they went to it with listless indifference, or the sullen determination to escape all of the task which they could. They accomplished their work as it was driven from them; not by the lash, but by fear of passing the night upon the bare iron bars of their bed-frame; or the stone floor of the solitary cell, without covering beside their ordinary dress, without food, save the daily slice of bread and quart of cold water.

Between the ringing of the bells the unlocking had been accomplished. One of the sweeps was stationed at the end of the upper tier of cells. When the second bell rung I called to her, —

"Slide your bar!"

The long bar that runs across the top of all the cells of one division, with a bolt reaching down over each door to keep it shut when it is unlocked, was then drawn out by her, so that the doors could be opened. I then called, —

"Third Division!"

At that they all appeared at their doors.

I called, "Front!"

The doors were opened, and they stood on the threshold.

"Right face!"   All wheeled to the right.

"March!" was the next order.

At that word they marched down the stairs, in the order that they came out of their cells, deposited the ration pan and quart, in which they had carried their supper to their rooms the night before, on the ration table, to be taken into the kitchen and washed, ready to receive their breakfast, which was passed out in them when they came in from work at seven.

The other divisions were called out in the same way, and followed in their order.

Unrefreshed, sleepy, and without energy, they moved along to their two hours of labor before breakfast. And such a breakfast to look forward to when it came. Rye coffee and mush, varied with brown bread once a week, and this purposely stinted to the least possible amount which one could subsist on and work.

I noticed that most of them took only their coffee, and worked upon that when it was brown bread morning till the noon meal came.

Many a one looked into her quart, as she passed me, and sighed out, "God help us!"

"May He help you! He only can — I cannot," was my response; but not always made audibly.

He only knew how I longed to do so. I often said to myself, as the days passed on, I would not starve a dumb dog as those poor human things are starved. I would not work a dumb animal as those poor human things are worked! **Nor would the** Master feed **his horse as they were fed ;** nor would he stall him as those prisoners were lodged.

I did **what I could for them. I asked the** Deputy if he could not substitute flour bread **for the** brown which they refused. He answered, —

" No ! **They** will come **to it. The Master will** not change the order."

They did not come **to it. And day after day, as I** saw them **go** breakfastless **to their work, I** wished, — was it wrong? perhaps so, — that the avenger might **be on the** track of that unfeeling Master, and that the **day** might come when **he** might **be** obliged to breakfast upon **a** quart of rye coffee **and a** slice of brown bread, instead of the steaks, **and** eggs, and toasts, and other delicacies that I saw carried to his room from the kitchen, **as** I passed through it to the officers' dining-room.

If it aroused **such** indignation **to** witness **such** cruelty, what must it **do in the hearts of** those **who** suffer from **it ! Does** such **correction of convicts** tend **to arouse better purposes in their hearts than** those which brought them **into** prison ? Such treatment aroused in them **anger** and **revenge.** When they dared, and **in** every way which they could invent without laying themselves liable to punishment, they gave expression **to** their feelings.

When they were dismissed from the prison, **the** officer usually remarked, **" We** shall have **that** boarder back again."

The answer that I should have made, had I spoken my thoughts, would have been — The whole tendency of their discipline here is to produce that end.

The first thing that I did, after breakfast was over, was to take the names of my six kitchen women, and learn, as nearly as I could, just what work belonged to each one of them.

There were two sink women, McMullins and Magill. Their work was to wash the dishes, keep the sink clean, and scrub about one quarter of the floor. The slide woman scrubbed the ration table, a certain portion of the floor, washed the quarts and piled them up, scrubbed the table in the centre of the room, took care of the flour bread when it came in, and the pieces that were left. At meal time she passed out the coffee, and put the potatoes in the ration pans.

The cook made the mush, which was boiled twice a day, the soup, and hash, and stewed the peas. She had a certain portion of the floor to scrub, and the room to keep tidy, as well as her boilers to wash.

The steam woman took care of the steam boiler, made the coffee, helped the cook slice the meat, and kept her portion of the floor clean. It was a part of her work to pile the ration pans in rows of pyramids on the centre table.

The one .who tended the women's slide had one half of the floor to scrub, and the Master's furnace, which stood in the centre of the kitchen, to tend.

There were many things to be done in common, where all helped; like the carrying out of the swill, which was emptied into tubs when the ration pans came in to be washed. That was carried a long way down the yard, poured into barrels, and left for the yard man to take to the piggery.

They all helped to bring up the potatoes, four barrels at a time, wash them in the sink with a large bat-stick, and then put them in the boiler to be cooked by steam.

To make the confusion more confounded, the work was changed round, and new hands put to it, the day I went there. The bringing up of the coal, for the steam boiler, which had heretofore devolved upon the steam woman, was now required of all the rest, to be divided among them, because the steam woman had had a broken wrist, and it was not quite strong again. That gave dissatisfaction, and created grumbling, and the constant contention of shifting the labor from one to the other. The rest were constantly fretting Allen, the steam woman, because she asked it of them.

To settle the difficulty I asked the Deputy, when he came round, — " who should bring up the coal for Allen ? "

" Any of them that you see fit to order."

That was an excellent hint to me. Allen had been in the habit of giving her own orders, which made it necessary for me to interfere continually so as to get them executed, and also to keep peace

They invariably answered her back with refusal when she asked for coal, and made altercation over every bucket that was needed.

All orders, like information, were given promiscuously. I at once gave direction that all orders were to be given through me.

"Allen, when you wish for coal, come to me for it!"

Orders had no authority when given by one to another; and by watching I discovered that Allen was disposed to retaliate the little peckings she received, by making the one that aggravated her most bring up the most coal.

It was more than one day's work to bring them to this arrangement. So I made it another rule that when they differed they were never to answer back; but come to me to settle the trouble. That was rather more difficult to establish than the first, they were so hot-headed, and anxious to defend themselves.

O'Sullivan, one of the slide women, undertook to try my authority on the first order which I gave for coal. She sat idly upon her table, and I asked her to bring it up.

A scowl came over her face, she hesitated, and then answered, —

"She's just as well able to bring up the coal as I."

"That's so! that's so!" came from three or four other voices.

"Stop! every one! It is the order that Allen is

not to bring up coal; you have nothing to say about it."

The others were silenced.

"O'Sullivan, will you bring up a bucket of coal?"

"I'm not going to bring up her coal; she's as well able to fetch it up as I."

"You will do just what I tell you! Go now and bring a bucket of coal!"

She started, after looking me in the eye a few seconds to see whether she could succeed if she attempted to disobey.

"When you come back I will talk with you about it."

I must have prompt obedience. I saw that her condition, that of motherhood, required consideration.

While she was gone Allen came to me and whispered, —

"They never lock up women like her, so she takes the advantage."

After she had brought up the coal, and sat down upon the table again, I went along to her, laid my hand upon her shoulder, stooped down, and said softly, —

"I see the condition that you are in, — I know that it requires care, — I am a mother, — I will see that you do no more than your part. You will do as I wish in future, pleasantly, will you?"

"Yes, ma'am!"

I then called them all around me, and said to them, —

"The bringing up of the coal for the steam boiler is to be divided among you. I will give each her share of it to do as equally as I can. If any one of you thinks she is doing more than belongs to her, rightfully, make no talk about it, but come directly to me, and I will see that it is made right."

My first object was to lead the women to make me the central, regulating power, in the kitchen, so that I could reduce the chaotic state of affairs to something like order.

"In a week," I said to the Deputy that day, "I hope to get something like order established."   .

"I will give you a month to get the run of things."

"You want the meals well cooked, and promptly passed out at the time; the place kept quiet and clean."   .

"That is what we want."

"Be patient, and in a week or two we shall arrive at that."

"I shall find no fault till I see occasion."

That night, after the work was done, I called them all around me, and told them they would find me kind and pleasant, if they were obedient. If they were not, they would surely find themselves in trouble, because it was a part of my duty to make them obey, and it must be done by the rules of the institution; I could not change them. I saw that their work was hard; but I would make it as easy as possible. The work was there, and they were put there to do it. The more willingly they undertook it, the easier it would go off. If they tried to help themselves, I would help them.

They all assented, and thus we made a compact to be kind to each other.

3

IV.

A QUARREL, AND DISCIPLINE.

It was my third morning in prison. I stood beside the mush boiler with Annie O'Brien, who had been scraping it, and was wiping it out with a dry cloth.

McMullins came along, and demanded the cloth from her. An altercation ensued. I hushed the noise, and asked, —

"To whom does the cloth belong?"

"It is my dish-cloth," said McMullins.

"You might let me have it a moment just to wipe this out!"

"I want it meself, I'm in hurry for it."

"Where is yours?" I asked O'Brien.

"I don't know, ma'am. I left it on the boiler, and some one has taken it."

She still kept on using McMullins'.

"I want my dish-cloth; I'm in hurry," said Mc-Mullins, impatiently.

"Give her the dish-cloth, and go find your own!" I said.

Annie O'Brien's temper was like a lucifer match.

At the command she threw the cloth in McMullins's face.

Quick as a cat would spring upon a mouse, McMullins was upon her ; and the report of the slaps that fell quick, and followed each other fast on the side of O'Brien's face, sounded through the room.

It was in vain that I called upon them to stop. O'Brien was enraged. She caught up an iron rod that lay upon the window seat, and struck McMullins a blow upon her forehead that brought blood.

I called the other women to the spot, and they were soon parted.

I sent McMullins out of the room, took O'Brien, who was white with anger, by the arm, and led her to a seat.

" Sit down ! "

She looked defiance for a moment; then, did as I commanded her.

" What kind of behavior is this, Annie O'Brien ? " I asked, sternly.

" She slapped me in the face — slapped in the face by that low hussy ! "

The thought added fuel to her rage, and she started up again as though to pursue her.

" Be quiet ! "

She sat down again. I stood silent by her.

" She slapped me in the face ; by ——, I will not bear it ! "

She darted past me, and caught up a carving-knife that lay on the table.

" She slapped me in the face ; and, by ——, I will have her heart's blood ! "

My heart sickened at the disgusting scene ; but my duty was before me.

" Stop her, and take the knife away ! " I shouted to the women at the other end of the room.

In a moment the knife was taken from her, and both of her hands were confined by four of the women.

" Annie O'Brien, come here ! " I called.

She looked at me, but did not stir.

I called again, " Annie O'Brien, come here ! "

She said to the women that held her, " Let me go ! I will go to her," and she started towards me.

I laid my hand on her pale, cold cheek.

" O'Brien, are you not ashamed to get so angry with that poor, foolish, half-crazed Mullins ? "

" Wouldn't it make your blood boil to have any one slap you in the face ? "

" Undoubtedly it would rouse my temper for the moment. It is a very mean and wrong thing to strike ; but you have behaved no better."

" I was a fool ; but I could not help it."

" Yes, you could. Will you behave yourself now ? "

" I will do nothing more," and she heaved a deep sigh.

" If you have really come to your senses, go about your work ! "

She returned to her work ; but in a moment she called to me, —

" You must report me ! "

" Yes, in my own time."

" You must report me now; I must be punished. They will blame you if you put it off."

" Would you care if they blamed me, Annie " ?

" Yes, ma'am, I should. It is bad enough for me to behave so without making you any more trouble."

" I wish to see you entirely over your frenzy, perfectly quiet, before I call the Deputy."

" I am perfectly quiet," and she went about making her mush.

" Annie, if you will promise me to try to control your temper in future, I will try to get your punishment made as light as possible."

" I will try to do anything you want me to; but they will put it on to me hard, I've been punished so many times before."

I saw that I had possession of her so far as she had control of herself.

" Keep about your work as though nothing had happened ! "

" Yes, ma'am."

I went to the door, blew my whistle, and sent for the Deputy. I waited in the entry for him, and stated the case before he went in to punish the women.

" McMullins gave the first blow; you know she is a poor, foolish thing; she has fits. You won't punish her this time, will you? She slapped O'Brien in the face, and she struck back. Won't you let them off this time?"

"I can't. It won't do."

"Wouldn't it make you angry, and wouldn't you strike back if any one struck you in the face?"

"Probably I should."

"You won't punish her for doing what you would do yourself?"

"I must."

"If one is punished both must be. The trouble began in Annie's not having her own things to use. I will see that each has her own things in future, and avoid cause of contention in that way as much as possible. If McMullins should have a fit in her cell, we should both feel bad. Can't you let them off with a reproof this time?"

"I can't. McMullins must not count on the fool's pardon when she fights. If I let her go now she might fly in any woman's face at any time. They never would be safe from her slappings. Don't you think they ought to be punished?"

"Yes, sir; with some kind of punishment."

"If I were to let them off, it would be known all through the prison in two hours, and there would be rebellion in all quarters."

"Subordination must be maintained. I wish there were a different way. I am so sorry to have the poor things locked up."

"I am sorry; but I have no other way."

When he went into the kitchen, Annie O'Brien

took off her apron, and delivered herself up to him
without a word; but McMullins cried, and begged
him not to lock her in a black cell.

He made no reply, but pointed them to the prison.
As he went, he asked me to bring No. 1 key.

The black cells are of the same size, and made
like the others. The only difference between them
is, that the doors of the black cells are closed from
the entrance of all light by a black board placed
against the bars.

They have no beds in them, not a blanket to lie
upon. Nothing but the cold stones to sit, to stand
upon, or to lean against. The only article of furni-
ture allowed in them is the night bucket, which may
be converted into a seat. The rations, when in that
" durance vile," is one quart of water, and one thin
slice of bread during the twenty-four hours.

With a heavy heart I saw my poor women locked
up. I turned the key upon them with my own hand.

O this continual turning of keys! The bunch in
my hand all day, under my pillow at night.

Click, click, when I go out of the room; click,
click, when I come in. Will my ears ever harden
to the sound so that I shall not notice it!

It is a constant drill, drill to labor under the ever
impending punishment, which hangs over the prisoner, suspended by a breath of complaint by an officer. Is one kind of punishment the only cure for disobedience? Should it not be mitigated by mercy, or
changed in character according to the circumstances,

or the peculiar disposition of the offender? How does the Great Lawgiver treat His convicts? Does He punish all offenders with the same unmitigated rigor? His sun shines alike on the evil and the good. He reproves often, and teaches, and suffers long, and is kind, and adapts His punishment to the character of the crime committed.

Some crime is committed in willful disobedience of known law; but much more of it in ignorance of the way to control bad tempers — in ignorance of the way to resist temptation.

Teaching is what these poor creatures want, and the time in which to learn.

Many a time I went to the key-holes of those black cells to listen that day. Many a time I called, —

" McMullins, are you well ?"

She invariably begged me to let her out.

" I cannot. You did wrong and must be punished."

" She threw the dish-cloth at me."

" You struck her."

" I'll never do it again, I am so tired. Please will you get the Deputy to let me out."

" Just as soon as I can."

That night I went to him, and begged to have my women let out.

" You know McMullins has fits, and to lie there on the cold stones all night might bring them on."

" You may put her in her own room to sleep."

" Thank you ! It is a favor done to me as well as

her. I don't think I could sleep at all if she were left lying there. You will let O'Brien go to hers — it would be hardly right to let one sleep in her bed, and not the other."

He shook his head.

"O'Brien has been here before. I know more about her than you do."

"Let me try her my way, Mr. Deputy?"

"Not to-night."

"In the morning?"

"I will see."

O'Brien was obliged to make the cold stones her couch that night, and little sleep did I get thinking of her. Many a time did I say to myself in its silent hours, I will have her out in the morning if it is in the power of persuasion to effect it.

After the women were locked up, Annie called to me. Her quick ears had learned, or some other prisoner had told her, that McMullins was in her own cell.

She asked, —

"Is it right to keep me in here, and let McMullins sleep in her bed?"

It was not for me to decide the right or wrong of the Deputy's orders, to a prisoner.

"McMullins has fits, and it would not be safe to leave her in solitary all night. I should not sleep at all if she were there. I am sorry for you, O'Brien; but you don't wish McMullins to remain, in solitary because you must, do you?"

" No, ma'am ; but it don't seem hardly fair to let one out, and not the other."

She was using the same argument with me to get her bed that I had used with the Deputy to get it for her.

" When you have been here before, and been punished, you have behaved very badly, have you not ? "

" Yes, ma'am."

" Annie O'Brien, will you be patient to-night, and make no complaints ? "

" Yes, ma'am."

" In the morning, when the Deputy comes around, will you tell him that you will try to govern your temper ? "

" I will tell you so."

" Will you tell him so ? "

" Yes, ma'am."

" Good night, Annie, and may the Christ, whose name you called so wickedly this morning, take care of you ! "

" Good night, ma'am ! "

The next morning, when I gave O'Brien her bread and water, I asked her,—

" O'Brien, do you think, if McMullins were to strike you again, you would strike back ? "

" I don't think I should now, — I shouldn't if I thought."

" What do you think of your behavior yesterday ? "

" I am ashamed of myself that I should take any notice of that poor, foolish, half crazy thing ! But

I've got an awful temper, and it gets the upper hands of me before I know it."

" When the Deputy comes around, if he says anything to you, will you tell him you are ashamed of yourself, and resolved to do better ? "

" He never could make me say it to him before."

" He may not ask you to now; if he does, you will be submissive and perfectly respectful ? "

" Yes, ma'am, I will."

When the Deputy came in, I importuned him to unlock my women.

" If I do, it will only be to have O'Brien locked up again in a few days. She has been here twice before, and is one of the worst cases we have ever had."

" If she is subdued and promises to do better, is not that enough ? "

" Subdued ! " he echoed. " She will promise anything to get out."

" Did you ever get a promise from her to do better ? "

" I don't think we ever did. She has always braved us as long as she could speak."

" I am a new mistress, my management may be new to her. Will you let me try her, if you please ? She is such a young thing, it seems as though she might be influenced to reform. You are punishing me to keep her in that dark cell. It takes my strength all away to think of her there. I could not sleep last night, — thoughts of her haunted me."

The tears came into my eyes. If he had refused me, I should have cried outright. He was a man, and one of kindly feelings, too, when left to himself. He gave me the order,—

"Bring me your key!"

I brought it very quickly, and unlocked Annie's cell with more alacrity than I ever turned key in a lock before.

"O'Brien," said the Deputy to her, "I let you out because your Matron asks me to. Now show your gratitude by your good behavior, and obedience to her."

"I will try, sir."

"Unlock the other one when you please," he said to me, and went out.

O'Brien turned to me.

"I will never give you occasion to have me locked up again, while I am here. I never made the promise before, but I make it now. I have been in solitary ten days and ten nights; I have been carried from there to the hospital, fainted away dead, and my feet so swelled that I could not walk on them. I have been gagged till my jaws were so stiff and swelled that I could not shut my mouth. I have been in the dungeon in the cellar "—

"Stop, Annie! in the name of pity, stop!"

I was sick to loathing of the cruelty she recounted. Was I in one of the prisons of the Inquisition, hearing a description of their tortures?"

"It is the truth. And I never made a promise to do any better before."

I trembled with disgust, almost fear, of the place I was in. I bethought me, I am here to benefit these poor wretches. I held my breath as I asked,—

"What was all that done for?"

"Because I sauced a matron, and wouldn't say I was sorry."

"Did you say it at last?"

"No, ma'am! I wouldn't have said it if they had killed me. I was so mad I had just as soon died as not. The more they did to me, the madder I grew, and I swore, if ever I should catch her outside, I would pay her back, if I got in here for life."

"Annie O'Brien, if you were to sauce me, as you call it, I should punish you." I did not say how. "I expect you to treat me with respect always. It is not treating me with respect to quarrel with the other women in my presence."

"I shall always treat you with respect. I could never be mean enough to do anything else after the way you have treated me."

She fulfilled her promise. Never yet have I met a human being that kindness would not influence; but I have met with many a perverse will that harshness would neither bend or break.

"Now, Annie, you say that you wish to govern your temper, and that you will try?"

"I will try!"

"I will help you. When you begin to grow angry, shut your lips close together; then, look for me before you answer."

" I will, if I can think."

" As soon as you do think, come straight to me,
and tell me that you were getting angry. If I see
you, and can catch your eye, I will lift my finger in
warning; or I will call your name. Will you heed
me ? "

" I will try, with all my might."

" Go get your breakfast, and then go about your
work."

Many a time after that, when I saw her face grow-
ing pale with anger, I have called her name, and
lifted my finger. She would recognize the signal,
drop upon a bench, or the bare brick floor, bury her
face in her hands for a few moments, then arise and
go about her work without speaking a word.

Once, about a week after that locking up, she got
into an altercation with the slide woman. I was in
the prison; but I heard her voice, and ran to the
kitchen door.

" Annie ! " I called. She did not heed me, but went
on with her dispute. " Annie, remember ! " I whispered in her ear as I caught her arm.

She jerked it away from me. I looked her steadily in the eye. She dropped hers. She was waver-
ing between the disposition to obey, and the desire
to indulge her temper.

" There is the Dr.'s whistle, Annie. Run to the
wash-room, and tell Mrs. Martin he is coming ! "

She ran out quickly; but when she came back,
she walked slowly, looking down to her feet. She
came up to me and asked : —

" Why didn't you get me punished? I almost broke my promise; but I didn't mean to. If you had scolded me, I certainly should."

" I did not get you punished, because I see that you are trying to govern your temper, and I promised to help you. If I were to get angry and scold, of what use would it be for me to reprove you?"

" If you had scolded me then, I should certainly have sauced you, and then I should have been punished. Didn't you send me away on purpose?"

" If I did, it was better than scolding."

" I thought so; and this shall be the last time I will be so foolish."

" I hope so; but if I am obliged to hold up my finger a great many more times, I shall not be disappointed."

V.

THE SUPERVISOR, AND THE RULES.

As my orders conflicted, and my work bothered me, I made another effort to find a head manager, or some printed regulations.

When the Deputy came in, on his morning rounds, I asked him, —

"Is the Master's wife Head Matron here?"

"Yes."

"Then why does she not come and teach me to manage my department, and see that I do my duty? I go to you, and you tell me the other matrons know. I go to them, and they tell me so many conflicting things that I am bothered more than helped. Then if I ask some of them one thing, they wish to manage the whole, and come in, and give orders that produce such an effect that I am obliged to give others to countermand them. They give them in such a way, too, that my women are all stirred up, and it takes me a long time to get them settled down again. This morning, one of them told Mrs. Martin that she needn't come in here putting on airs, and giving off orders, when she was no better than the rest of them. I pretended not to hear it, for I really thought she provoked the answer. If there is a Head Matron, she ought to come to my rescue."

" The Master's wife is Supervisor," said the good-natured fellow, after thinking a few moments. He was anxious to make it right on her part.

Superfudge! I thought to myself. I said, —

" I wish she would supervise my place into order. Have you any printed directions ? "

" Yes. I don't think they would do you much good, but I will bring them to you."

He did not offer to bring the Supervisor to me, or to take me to her. As I got acquainted with the affairs of the institution, I found that she was emphatically super to all of them except her own housekeeping. She had brilliancy enough to look after that, and see that it was done well. She had the ability, and she exercised it, to come or send down when her parlor, which was directly over the prisoners' kitchen, was too cold, to have the furnace door shut, or if it was too warm, to have it opened.

About a week after I went there she came in, probably my repeated inquiries had been reported to her, and gave me an order to have a room cleaned in the attic of the prison. It was one morning when we were in the midst of house-cleaning with a gang of men whitewashing in the prison.

I told her I didn't think it possible to attend to it that day.

" I will show it to you now, because I have time."

I really had not time to look at it, as any one of

4

common powers of observation would have seen ; but, as she was my superior officer, I followed her without farther remark.

As she passed through the prison, and saw the men at work, she gave me another illustration of her luminous capacity by remarking, —

" You must be careful and not let your women get with the men."

" Yes, ma'am."

She took me up the sixth flight of stairs into the roof of the prison, into a room where the receiving officer packs away the clothing that he takes off the convicts when they come into the prison. After showing me the dust on the floor, and cobwebs on the walls, she said, —

" You had better send one of your women up to clean it. I always begin at the top when I clean house."

" I don't see how I can spare one to-day. If the Deputy will send me in one to do it, I will do my best to oversee it. But you see how inconvenient that will be, it is so far up here, and there is so much going on in the kitchen."

" It won't be much to clean this."

I thought, but did not say it, it might appear differently to you if you were to do it. I should consider it a good day's work for two strong women.

I looked round with her, and listened to her suggestions.

" What I wanted to call your attention to, particularly, was this box of old clothes. I think it must have been here two or three years."

I wondered if it had been two or three years since she had been in that room.

"They are cloth caps," she went on, "there may be an old coat or pair of pants among them. I don't think they will be of any use, — they might as well be sold, and the pay go towards the support of the institution."

I looked into the box. There might have been twenty pounds of woolen rags, originally; but they were nearly chowdered into dust by moths.

I saw by that one interview the occasion of the reticence of the Deputy, with regard to the Head Matron.

The first moment of leisure I got, that afternoon, I examined the printed " Rules and Regulations," by the Board of Directors, which the Deputy had brought me. They were printed eight or ten years before, but sensible and humane so far as they went.

There were no directions to regulate the details of duty; but all of the Master's orders were subject to the approval of the Board. I did not see how it could be possible to carry that article out, practically, when many of them were changed almost every day.

One order that I noticed gave me great satisfaction, and had it been observed, would have created a very different state of things in the prison from what then obtained. It was, that " no irritating language " should be used to the prisoners. Had that rule been observed, there would have been comparatively few " in solitary," to the number which came under my observation.

I came to the conclusion that if the rules which governed the institution had been subjected to the approval of the Board of Directors, that august body must entertain a very imperfect idea of their practical working.

One of my orders was to stand at the ration table, in the kitchen, while the meals were passed out. Another was to be in the prison, at the same time, on duty, which shut me out of the kitchen entirely.

The trouble that arose from the conflicting orders was this. After I left the kitchen, the food for the meals was under the control of the prisoners, and they secreted what part of it they pleased for themselves and their favorites.

Before I left the kitchen I saw the meat sliced, and an equal portion placed in each pan. After I left, and there was no one to watch it, the women abstracted a part of it from some of the pans, or changed it from one pan to another.

I was allowed about two hundred and eighty pounds of meat for the four hundred prisoners, bones included. After this was sliced, it was divided to each pan as nearly equally alike as possible. To this was added three or four potatoes, with the skins on, and the gravy or soup was then poured over them.

These pans were arranged in rows across the ration table, to be passed out, through a slide, to the men, as they were marched into prison, on their side; and to the women, on their side. The kitchen was between the prisons.

After the pans were arranged on the table, and the dinners put into them, I was obliged to go out into the prison to receive the women, and see them slid into their cells. The slide door was shut upon me, and the convicts were left alone with the food to hand it out.

Was it strange, with this opportunity placed in their way, that they should help themselves to the meat which had been divided to the others?

My order was to detect the thief and report her. That was much easier said than done. My opinion was that they all took it.

It was a question strongly debated in my mind, who was most at fault, those poor, half-starved things, for taking the meat when the opportunity was given them, or those who put the temptation in their way?

I did not decide it in season to have any of them punished for breaking the rule.

When the convicts got angry, with each other, they would report on the one they were offended with; but it was an established rule that the testimony of one prisoner was not to be taken against another, and I had not the least inclination to break the rule.

I did discover one of the thieves at last; but I took my own way to punish her.

The steam woman got angry with one of the slide women, and reported her to me one day when the dinner came short.

" Never mind now, Allen ; but the next time you
see her take it, tell me where she hides the meat. I
will go find it ; and then, she can't turn it on you for
betraying her."

A day or two afterwards, Allen whispered to me, —

" You look on the top of the bread closet in the
cellar, and you will find something."

I went down, mounted some false steps, and found
a quart filled with slices of meat. I took it up into
the kitchen, and asked, —

" Who hid this meat away on the top of the bread
cupboard in the cellar ? "

Not one of them answered.

" Will the one who did it be honest enough to own
it ; or will she be mean enough to let me lay the
blame on some one else? Did you do it, Annie
O'Brien ? "

" No, ma'am."

" Will you tell me who did it ? "

" I don't know, ma'am."

" Allen, did you do it ? "

" No, ma'am."

I did not wish to ask her who did it, because she
had told me.

" I am going to ask you all, and I hope no one will
be mean enough to lie about it."

" I put it there," said O'Sullivan.

" Who did you put it away for ? "

" For myself, because I don't like peas."

" Very well, O'Sullivan ; but you were rather too

generous to yourself. Half of that would have been enough for your dinner, and to punish you for being so selfish, you can't have any of it. I shall give it to the others. Your hiding it away down there, gave it very much the appearance of stealing. In future, when you wish to put anything away, show it to me, and then, put it away like an honest woman. But you are never to put anything away unless it is left over, after I have divided the meat. It would be very mean to take a double portion for yourself, and make the poor fellows, on the other side go without."

I had been studying the Rules and Regulations of the Board, and discovered that I was to admonish once, before reporting for punishment. I did not propose to transcend that rule.

" Now, remember, there is nothing more to be hid away from me."

" There isn't much danger, as long as you let us tell you all about it."

" I shall always let you tell me, before I get you punished ; but you must always obey, and then there will be no punishment."

" I suppose it is only right that we should eat our share of peas with the rest, for they can't get even bread and coffee as we can."

" It is certainly wrong for you to take another prisoner's meat ; and very mean, because, as you say, he has not the chance you have to get anything else. Now, girls, will you promise not to hide things away, and try to cheat me any more ? "

"I will, I will," was responded by the six. I did not expect them to do it without a great many more "admonishings."

"Now, girls, be on your guard, so that the temptation does not become too strong for you."

When the Deputy came in, I asked him whether the order for me to stand at the ration table in the kitchen, at meal time, had been approved by the Board.

"Of course it has."

"Has the order for me to be on duty in the prison at meal time, been approved by the Board?"

"Certainly!"

"You consider them a very intelligent body of men, do you not?"

"Of course, — they are my superior officers."

"How can they expect me to be in two different places at the same time?"

"I really don't know much about the arrangements on the women's side at meal times. My station is in the men's prison at that time."

"Yes, sir; and it is the place of our head officer to be stationed on this side, in the women's prison, at that time, and it is my place to be in the kitchen at meal time, to see that the meals go out properly, and that none of them are turned from the right channel."

The next day afforded him an illustration of what I said. The dinner fell short. He entered the kitchen at one door as I went in at another. He came hurrying up to me, and asked — " Why is this ? "

" I don't know, sir! It was all right when I left the kitchen. Since that, I have no means of knowing what has been going on. I have been shut out in the prison, on duty."

He ordered in bread to supply the deficiency. In that case it was the mismanagement of the hash, by a new hand, when " dished out," which would have been prevented had I been there to oversee it.

VI.

FIRST NIGHT ALONE IN PRISON.

The four Matrons took the evening watch, alone in prison, in rotation. It was a rule that one of them was to be always there, when the prisoners were in. They were not to be left by themselves a moment.

The one who had charge was to be alone; the other three were at liberty, one to go about the buildings or grounds, two to go out of the prison confines, if they liked. It was my turn to be alone in prison.

Immediately after they had been locked into their cells, and the other Matrons had left, Haggerton began to complain of her coffee.

"What is the matter with your coffee?" I asked.

"It is cold," she replied.

"I am sorry; but I can't help it now."

Upon that she began to fret. "I haven't eaten any breakfast, nor any dinner, and I've worked hard all day, and staid an hour later," — some of them had staid till eight o'clock that night in the shop — "and now I can't eat any supper because my coffee is cold. I'll tell the Master, and he'll make an awful fuss."

Of course I could not allow such talk as that, and I told her to stop.

" I have done the best for you that I could. You had the same chance to eat that the rest had, and the same breakfast and dinner provided for you. I am not allowed to provide anything else. If you haven't eaten, it is your own fault."

" I can't eat brown bread, and I can't eat soup, nor I can't drink cold coffee. The Master will be awful mad, and make an awful fuss, for me to have cold coffee."

" Not another word, Haggerton ! If you don't like the fare, you ought not to take board here," I said. I thought, if the Master would feel so bad that your coffee is cold, why don't his compassion lead him to provide something that you can eat.

Upon that she went on to cry and sob, and make a great disturbance in the prison.

I told her she must stop ; but she kept on. I had not the heart to scold and threaten the girl. I had no doubt that she was tired and hungry, and I pitied her. I went for the Deputy, to see what I should do. He was out. I stepped into the officers' dining-room to find some one to direct me.

Mrs. Hardhack, the Shop Matron, was eating her supper. The Supervisor sat there, talking with her. I stated the case to her. Before I had got half through with it, she motioned me away, and ex- claimed, in great agitation, —

" You mustn't leave the prison alone a moment! You mustn't leave the prison alone a moment! "

Mrs. Hardhack rushed past me as though every prisoner had got loose, and was running away.

I thought they would probably be safe if she arrived without accident, and followed at my usual gait.

When I entered the prison she was leaving Haggerton's cell door, and from the second division saluted me with, —

"It's no wonder the girl cries! her coffee is cold! I went to the kettle and tasted it myself! She hasn't eaten a mouthful to-day; and now, to have cold coffee given her for her supper, it's too bad! The Master shall know it, and he'll make an awful fuss."

I made no reply to her; but the next morning, I had several questions to ask the Deputy.

"It is a rule, is it, that the prisoners are not to be left alone a moment at night, after they are locked in?"

"Yes."

"Then how am I to leave the prison, go across the kitchen, and pass out my keys? Sometimes it will be ten or fifteen minutes before I can make the prison officer hear my rap."

"Of course you must do that."

"Then I must leave the prison alone. Have the Board of Directors approved both those rules?"

He smiled.

"The reason why I asked was, because the Supervisor and Shop Matron thought I had committed a great violation of the rules, to leave the prison a moment to find you, to ask you a question, when I was in difficulty last night."

"Did you have any difficulty last night?"

I told him the story of Haggerton, and Mrs. Hard-hack's management in the case.

"You can judge that such conduct is calculated to produce disorder, and it did. It was nearly half an hour before I got the women quiet again."

"Mrs. Hardhack has been here many years — she ought to know better than to behave in that way. If she don't, I can teach her."

I did not tell him what followed. I had been studying the " Rules and Regulations " of the Board of Directors, for myself, and intended to abide by them. I remarked carelessly, —

"The Board direct that the convicts shall work from sunrise to sunset. They were worked an hour later last night."

"They had some contract work that they wanted to finish."

"The order of the Board is to work from sunrise to sunset. There is no provision made for finishing contract work. The order to work over hours was submitted to the Board for approval last night, was it not?"

"You are sharp. I see you wish to do your own duty, and you wish others to do the same."

"Yes, I like to do my duty if I can find out what it is. In this particular case, I am indifferent whether others do theirs or not. But, if I find them follow-ing me up to make me perform mine accurately, when they are involved in the same, it is perfectly natural for me to turn and observe their manner of doing theirs."

"I am trying to do mine."

"I see that you are, and I am glad that you have a better opportunity to find out what it is, than I do."

The moment that Mrs. Hardhack was out of the prison, that night, the convicts commenced hooting and whistling. If she did not put Haggerton up, directly, to play off on me, which I strongly suspected, her behavior was calculated to encourage their conduct.

I was a new Matron, this was my first night alone, and they would try me, to see what stuff I was made of.

If Mrs. Hardhack had instigated their conduct, the punishment would come upon them, not her. It was my business to suppress the noise, and to detect those who were engaged in making it.

I drew my feet from my slippers, and commenced my search for the culprits.

It was made a short one by the assistance of one of the sweeps who hated Mrs. Hardhack, and would do anything to thwart her — even betray a fellow-prisoner.

She pointed me to one of the doors from whence the whistling came. I crept softly along, in the shade, and stood by the next door a moment. The girl, unconscious that I was near, gave another shrill call.

"That is you, is it, Kate Connolly?" I said, close to her ear.

She burst into tears at the sound of my voice. Her imagination at once brought before her the long aching induced by solitary confinement. It was far from an agreeable prospect to look forward to.

"I'm sorry! indeed I am!"

"Sorry for what, — that you made disturbance, or that I found you out?"

"For both. Indeed I am; I knew better — I knew the rules; I've been here before, and it'll go hard with me."

"You thought I was a stranger and wouldn't know them, did you?"

"Yes, ma'am; but I'm sorry."

"I'm sorry for you, Kate, that you should be so ill-disposed as to make a noise, purposely to disturb me; and that you should be so mean as to try to impose upon a stranger. In future it will be well for you to know who you are playing off on before you begin. Now, Kate Connolly, remember — if ever I catch you in another such a trick, I shall have you punished"!

"And you wont now? I thank you! I never will trouble you so again!"

I never had occasion to reprove her afterwards for any bad conduct while she was in the prison.

She thought it was through my kindness that she escaped punishment. I had been reading the "Rules and Regulations," which directed me to "admonish" once; and then, report for punishment. By following those Rules, I had silenced the noise, and restored order without resorting to punishment. I had also secured the future good behavior of the girl.

When one was detected, the others became quiet.

There are good and noble qualities still existing in those prisoners, if the right management only be applied to rouse, and bring them into action. The rule to admonish was a wise one, and was adopted to that end. That the officers did not follow out the rule was wherein the fault lay. And that they overlooked it, or failed to obey it, caused untold suffering to the prisoners.

No instance came under my observation where the offense was repeated, after a prisoner had been admonished.

After quiet was restored, I sat down to think, and rest. I was tired of the ceaseless surveillance, the turning of keys, the grating of bars, the driving of the prisoners at their tasks, the compelling to pleasant manners while under such severe exactions of toil.

I sat thinking it over and asking myself if it would be possible for me, driven, urged to work with no alternative but the solitary cell, and the bread and water diet, with no motive but fear of punishment, to be gentle and patient.

The exhausted flesh and the wearied spirit would express their agony in some form of complaint. Human nature might restrain its indignation at such a dreary lot from breaking forth, in fear of a greater punishment. The prisoner might work on in silence till she fell, and was carried to the Hospital. I was told that it had been so, and I could not doubt it.

My orders verified the statement. I was to keep them at work. If they complained they were to see the Doctor, and he was to decide whether they were unfit for labor. In that case they were to go into the Hospital.

I had asked, " Shall their whole task be exacted of them ? "

" Yes, — if you listen to their complaints, they will all play sick, and we shall get no work done."

I had said, "They might do something, and by not being driven so hard, made useful, and their health spared."

" We have no such rules," was the reply.

" But any Matron, after she is acquainted with her women, can judge so that they will not impose upon her very much."

" They will all cheat, and lie, and shirk, if they can."

That might be so generally ; but I knew that I had women who would rather work reasonably than be idle, because time passed faster when they were employed, if from no other motive.

If they would all lie, and cheat, and shirk, the discipline that was applied to them did not work any reformation in their characters.

The treatment meted out to them was hard, unremitting toil, enforced by harsh words and punishment.

Implicit obedience to arbitrary rules was exacted, with no reasons given why they were enforced, and no explanations for their necessity. The hard work, the solitary cell, the meagre food, the damp stone prison, the narrow cells, and the crawling vermin, all went in revision before me.

Can such discipline soften the heart, and turn its stern purposes to commit crime into the ways of virtue? Must not the hearts of these poor things inevitably grow harder under such influences, till they become the human fiends which they sometimes manifest themselves?

I looked along the whitewashed floor. Rats and mice were running fearlessly about, holding gay revel over the crumbs that had been scattered to them by the prisoners in their rooms.

I looked up at the cells. Human faces stared down upon me, through the bars, made ghastly by the flickering gas-light. There were human hearts, alive with all human emotions, beating beneath those horrid faces.

Directly in front of me, with no light, save one narrow, stinted ray, which glimmered through the key-hole, with no bed but the stone floor, no seat but the wooden bucket, nothing to lean against but the bare brick walls, lay a girl "in solitary."

No human being has life enough to stir up those cold stones to warmth, no change can soften them to comfort. Whichever way she turns, the hard, chilling granite is her resting-place. She lies there with no covering but her usual clothing, and that has been dealt out to her with the spare hand of public rigor.

No discretionary mercy has interposed to provide a plank or a blanket to break the chill.

Like a flash the thought crossed my brain, If that were my child! It sent a pang through my heart that stopped and wrung there till I gasped for breath.

I looked up at the cells. The faces that glared down upon me were the sweet faces of my own daughters transformed to human demons by the vile impress of crime, and its compeer, punishment.

Was I putting my hand to the work to help on the hardening of human hearts, and the degradation of human beings! I would flee the place, and leave the work with the morning light. I could not flee the thoughts. Wretched, wretched employment!

I was half frenzied. I started up and rushed around the prison. I laid my head against the iron bars of the grated doors. I leaned against the cold stone walls. I could have lain down upon them in bitter penance for the part which I had taken.

The eight o'clock bell rung for inspection. It was a relief.

Humbly I took my lantern, and crept softly round to examine the locks. Many of the women were in bed, some of them were up reading.

One of the girls looked up to me with a smile, and said, — I wondered that she could smile at all, —

" See how nicely I keep the rats out."

She had taken off the cover of her box, and braced it, by the box, against the lower part of the door.

Every room is furnished with a box which has a drawer in it. This box serves for table and pantry. It contains a spoon, knife and fork, salt and pepper boxes.

" Can't they jump over that?"

" They don't try ; but run along to another room. There hasn't been one in here since I put it up."

I sat down and busied myself reading till the nine o'clock locking came. When that was accomplished, I went up, up, up the stone stairs to my cell in the roof of the prison.

I laid me down, and from sheer exhaustion fell into a kind of slumber; but my short sleep, if it were sleep, was rank with nightmare, or haunted with the ghosts of my abode. No sooner did I become unconscious, than I was falling from my cyrie to the rocky floor below, or was strapped upon the iron bars that held the prisoners' beds. Visions appeared to my dream-sight that roused me with a start and scream to wakefulness again.

Even such disturbed slumber had hardly got possession of my faculties when a volley of oaths came rolling through my door, and roused me to distinct consciousness.

I sprang from my bed, ran to the door, and called. —

" What is the matter?"

" That bloody Smith snores so that we can't sleep !"

" Where is she? I will go down and wake her. "

" On the third division, south side, almost to the foot."

I put my feet into my slippers, wrapped a shawl around me, and ran down to Smith's door.

" Smith, turn over ! You are snoring so loud that the other women can't sleep."

" O ! how you scared me."

" Do you know that you are snoring so loud that the women can't sleep ? Turn over on your side ! "

" Yes, ma'am."

I went back to my bed, but no sooner had I settled myself to sleep than the clamor of complaint was renewed.

" That bloody Smith is at her snoring again !"

Again I started for the second division, south side.

" Smith ! you are snoring again ! "

" I can't help it, ma'am ! don't have me punished."

Punished ! How the idea haunted them, even in their sleep. " I know you can't help it, only by turning over. Turn on your face, and try that. The women must sleep, they are tired, and they are obliged to work to-morrow."

" I'll try not to snore, ma'am ! " She turned on her face as I directed her.

At last I attained to that state of repose which the renowned Sancho Panza has so felicitously eulogized, and successfully immortalized ; but my enjoyment was not of long duration.

It was but a short distance that reached into the

middle of the dark, dismal night, and time had travelled it when I slowly awoke. Shivers of terror, from some undefined cause, crept over me. Gradually I came to a knowledge of what was passing. My hair, which was thrown loosely over the pillow, was moving as though trodden by some nocturnal agent of locomotion. What moved it? there was no draft of air in the room.

I put my hand to the " crowning ornament by Nature given " to my head, and imprisoned a mammouth mouse, or scarce grown rat.

I was fast getting initiated into the mysteries of prison life, and inured to its peculiarities. Unmoved, I might allow my hair to become a bed for rats and mice ; but I could not spare the sleep.

I threw the creature from me, in a fret at being disturbed, and issued a peremptory order, independent of the Master, and without the approval of the Board, for all rats and mice to pay respect to my person, and my apartments, and trouble me no more. Then I turned over, and went to sleep again.

Adverse fate, or some other mysterious personage was on my track that night. Before I had time to close my eyes, a shrill shriek of horror resounded through the building, starting the echoes from every side.

It sounded in my ears like the despairing cry of one doomed to eternal death. Imagination supplied the cause, and brought me to my feet with one bound.

Some pent up prisoner was dying alone in his cell.
I sprang to the rail and called, —

" What is the matter ? "

" I think I had the nightmare. I do have it sometimes."

" Was that you, Mary McCullum? "

" I think it was, ma'am. I'm sorry I waked you !
Never mind me, ma'am ! "

Poor Mary McCullum ! In a moment I remembered all about her. They had told me a sad tale
about her incarceration for the murder of her rival.

Mary's husband had left her, taking her three little
girls away, and married another woman. Mary, in a
fit of jealous madness, had ground up a knife, enticed
the woman to drink with her, and murdered her in
her cellar. A policeman had detected her in the act.
God pity, and judge her ! She had been sentenced
to ten years of hard labor in the Penitentiary for the
crime.

Five years had been worked out. Her health was
gone, her nervous system had become a wreck. The
damp rooms, the chilling stones, the ceaseless toil,
were the slow torture that had undermined her constitution, and consumed her vitality.

Her narrow cell had become, to her imagination,
the home of demons who haunted her with her
crime.

The other women had told me that the ghost of
the murdered woman came to Mary McCullum every
night, all in her bloody garments, and set her shrieking in her dreams.

Should such a criminal go unpunished? The halter could bring no surer death than what was slowly creeping upon her. Restrained of her liberty she should be, and from the power to do further harm. Labor for her own support should be required of her. Connected with it, a sufficient amount of rest to secure health, a place to sleep free from the damp and noisome air of a stone prison.

A plenty of wholesome food should be allowed her; time and space for repentance given, time to think upon the error of her ways, and instruction that would teach her how to do it.

That worrysome night was to meet with one more "thrilling adventure" before it passed away into the light of the following day.

I lay, tossing from side to side, after I returned to my bed. Sleep was out of the question. I lay, tossing thoughts about the circumstances that surrounded me to and fro in my mind, trying to analyze, to distinctness, the mixed up conclusions that arose from them.

Another unearthly cry rung out on the air, and startled me from my perplexed meditations. It was more like the shriek of an animal in distress, than a human sound.

Wail followed wail, in quick succession. Can it be a human being? I asked myself, as I hurried on some clothing. It must be, there is nothing else here that can make such a noise.

I stopped to listen, as I went to search it out. It came from one quarter, and then, from another. If it were made in one cell, it possessed a wonderful power of ventriloquism.

I remembered the hooting and whistling of the night before, and immediately inferred that the same mischievous girls, who made the disturbance in the evening, had set up this cry and echoed it around from division to division, in order to make a night of it.

Quick as the thought entered my mind, my patience gave way. I vowed, in my heart, that I would have them punished if I could catch them. My own aroused temper certainly suggested the punishment that I contemplated. Even with the thought which suggested punishment arose the query — Is it not a just indignation that I feel, and do they not deserve punishment for willfully making this unreasonable disturbance ? Is it my anger that seeks revenge for the annoyance they are inflicting ?

Although half way down into the prison, I ran back to my room, and left my slippers, in order to avoid the tap, tapping of the leather soles on the walks, which would announce my approach to the culprits, and warn them in season to avoid detection.

Again I traversed flat after flat in my stockings. Quickly, and noiselessly, I threaded the walks towards the spot from whence the sound appeared to proceed. But when I reached it, all was silent there, and the wail came shrieking around another corner.

I grew more and more angry as chills crept up my

limbs, and set my teeth chattering. I raised my thinly clad feet from the cold stones only to set them down in a still colder track — a practical test, it now occurs to me, of the experience of the woman on the stones "in solitary,"— but my determination to ferret out the offenders never faltered.

I was benumbed ; but I persevered till I had traversed the five flats, and listened at the door of nearly a hundred cells. The wails had grown to howls, and filled the prison with their noise as the thunder fills the air with its reverberations, but eluded my search.

I gathered my shawl around me, and sat down by the stove to listen ; and determine my future course. When I became stationary, the sounds changed their course, and instead of receding approached me. Nearer, and nearer they came. In a moment they were issuing from the floor at my side. I shook with a vague dread. Were those shrieking wails from some prisoner confined in the dungeon vaults below the prison, insane or dying? Involuntarily I looked down. There stood the cat, uttering piteous cries on account of separation from her kittens in the kitchen, and pleading to be let out to them.

Quickly I ran over the stairs to get my keys, nor did I feel the chill of the cold stone walks, as I ran back to appease the distress of the mother cat by opening the way to her little ones.

I did not regret that I lost the opportunity to execute the mentally threatened punishment of my women.

VII.

ONE morning, as I sat warming my feet by the prison stove, I heard a slow, measured tread on the stone walk, like some one pacing off the length of the building. When it came near to me I looked, to see the Master stalking along in pompous dignity.

There was what he probably supposed to be authority in his bearing.

I arose and stood respectfully before him. I supposed he had commands of some kind, for me, from his appearance.

He went along without changing his gait, or turning his head, into the kitchen.

I really did not know what etiquette to observe on this state occasion; but I slowly followed him. He marched round, looking over the place in silent inspection; then came directly before me, and made a dead halt.

He did not speak for a moment, and I, to relieve the embarrassment, asked, —

" Does the place look to suit you ? "

" When it don't, I shall tell you," he answered gruffly.

" It is more pleasant to be told when we have pleased, than when we have not."

He made no reply to that remark ; but said sternly, —

" You are not to read the Rules to the prisoners ; you have nothing to do with that."

" I have not read the Rules to the prisoners. I can find no rules to be governed by myself, much more to read to them."

" If the prisoners do not obey you, you are to report them at once."

" I believe, according to the Rules and Regulations laid down by the Board of Directors, that I am to admonish them once, and at the second offense report them."

He turned and stalked away, looking a little puzzled.

At first I could not imagine to what he referred ; but after stirring up my memory, I recollected that I had mentioned, in reproving the women, a day or two before, that they were breaking the Rules.

I sat down and wrote the Master a note after this wise : —

" The women have a habit of talking as they march in and out of prison. I am ordered to report them if they do it. I find in the Rules and Regulations, given to the officers, by the Board of Overseers, on the tenth page, that we are directed to ' admonish ' the prisoners, for misbehavior, and at the second offense report them. That was what I did yesterday, however my proceedings may have been reported to you."

In a few moments the Deputy made his appearance.

"Your explanation was just the thing. We have looked up the Rule, and you are right. It is better to take each one as you catch her, rather than take them all together."

"That gives me a chance to exercise still more mercy. Thank you!"

Thus ended my first interview with the Master, and the second was like unto it.

About a week after that the Receiving Matron came and told me that I was to go to her wash-room, to oversee her women, while she went to put the officers' rooms in order.

I replied, "I cannot attend to your work. I have more to do in my own department than I have strength to accomplish."

"Mrs. Hardhack"— that was the Shop Matron — "said you were to do it."

"I am not employed by Mrs. Hardhack, nor do I take my orders from her."

I was overburdened with work, and extremely tired. It appeared unreasonable, to me, to crowd anything more upon me. I had not physical strength to do any more than I was doing.

The Matron turned from me in a fret, and left. I dropped upon a bench and rested my head upon the table. From sheer fatigue the tears started.

In a few moments I heard the measured tread of the Master. I did not raise my head till he had stood before me a moment or two. Then I looked up. I did not pay him the respect to rise. He looked at me a moment, and seemed to have some idea of my condition. He said gently, if anything could be said gently by one so rough —

"I should like to have you go to the wash-room while the Matron is at the officers' rooms. There is a gang of women at work there, and she cannot leave them alone very well."

His manner modified my feelings somewhat; but I had no idea of having any more labor put upon me, and I said, —

"I find it very difficult to get through with the labor that I engaged for, and it is impossible for me to have that of another put upon me."

"Just for to-day, as she has just come in."

"I will go for to-day, as a matter of favor; but I did not engage for that work, and I don't wish her to feel that she can call upon me to take her place at any time that she may wish. Her relief should come from another quarter."

"It is only for to-day."

He went out, and I started for the wash-house.

VIII.

MRS. HARDHACK.

I HAD been in the prison but a few days when Ellen, one of my "sweeps," crept softly round to me, and whispered in my ear, —

"You must be careful what you say! Mrs. Hardhack has just been in on the other side to listen. She creeps round like a cat, and you never know when she's coming, and there's no knowing what she'll tell, and she'll surely get you into trouble."

"Don't give yourself any uneasiness, she can't get me into trouble."

"Don't tell what I say; but she do pick a fuss with all the Matrons that come here, and she tells on 'em, and reports 'em, and makes the Master mad with 'em. And I jest see her creeping round in there now."

"You know that I am not obliged to stay here as you are, Ellen. If I am made unhappy, I can leave at any time."

"I know you can; but I don't want you to be unhappy. I want you to stay, and so do the rest of the women."

"Thank you, Ellen. I am glad you want me to stay, because I think you will do your work well and try to please me by obeying all of the rules."

"I'm sure I'll do anything in the world to please ye."

I thought I would see if Ellen's information were correct, so I stepped lightly around the corner to which she pointed. I was just in season to see the back of Mrs. Hardhack's garments disappearing through the door.

I was indifferent to such espionage personally. I could easily correct any false impression which might be made of my conduct, as I had done in the representation which had been made of my reading the Rules ; but it is extremely unpleasant to look upon such a character, as had been developed, in one who must be an associate. The meanness and treachery that were written upon it would stand out before me, whenever I saw her, in spite of any good qualities that she might possess.

That woman had been in the institution a great many years, and had become thoroughly imbued with the spirit of its rulers. If she went round into the other departments to listen, I inferred that it must be with the approval of the Master.

If she carried him information acquired in that way, it must be acceptable, or she would not continue it.

It is difficult to understand why such management need be pursued in this country. If the Master found a subordinate practicing against him, he could dismiss her arbitrarily ; but in so doing he would only dismiss her out into the world to tell her own tale, he would argue. He could make his own representation of the case to the Board of Directors, and screen his own doings; but the Board are not the directors of public opinion.

A just, upright, and open management would secure the coöperation of subordinates who are fit to hold a position in such an institution. That such a course was not pursued, was because the disposition of the head Manager led him in another direction, and the disposition of the subordinate, Mrs. Hardhack, made her a fit agent to carry out his peculiar views of the proper way to govern the institution.

She did not stop at that, but tried many little experiments of her own suggestion. Her long residence and knowledge of the place enabled her to practice them very much to the annoyance of the other Matrons, and to the distress of the prisoners.

The women were her equals in detecting her ways, if they had not the power to practice her stratagems.

They watched her till she was fairly across the yard that morning; then, they gathered around me, and began to tell me of her " tricks," as they called them.

" She's the artfulest huzzy that ever lived," said Ellen. " She'll tell the women when they leave the shop not to speak a word till they get out of it, nor in the yard; but when they get into the prison they may talk as much as they are a mind to. Don't ye see, that's to make you trouble. You'll have to scold 'em,

6

and get 'em locked up; and then, they'll hate you, and plague you all they can."

" Don't be anxious, Ellen? After I have been here awhile the women will understand me, and they won't be any more willing to plague me than you are."

" That's true! but it will take longer because you don't see 'em so much as you do us. And don't ye see, she'll tell 'em anything. She always be's stirring up a fuss somewhere. The women all hates her."

" Never mind saying anything more, Ellen. I think I can manage her."

" Don't let her know I've said anything! She'd surely pick up something to get me locked up for."

" 'Twas she that got me ten days in solitary, and the gag," said O'Brien. " I'd like to make her bones ache as mine ached then! If ever I catch her out-outside I'll " —

" Anne O'Brien, stop!"

" Well, ma'am, if she had treated you as she has me you would hate her. I'd strike her down in a minute if I could get the chance. And she will get struck down in the shop sometime and killed. She never goes outside, and she dares not, so many of the women hate her, and are on the watch for her."

That was the effect produced by solitary confinement, without mitigation, as I heard it talked universally among the prisoners. Does it conduce to reformation?

At the time this occurred, I thought the prisoners had exaggerated in their statements about Mrs.

Hardhack ; **but in a few** days **they** were confirmed **by her own** conduct.

I was suspicious that the truth had **been told me** with **regard to her putting the prisoners up to make a noise when they came in** prison, **by the** appearance **of a few of** them.

I thought I might arouse her pity for them, and **induce her to stop her machinations in** that way.

I remarked **to her, as we were standing** together **one** evening **after the women had been particularly noisy in coming in from the shop, —**

"I am afraid I shall **be obliged to have some of the women put in solitary if they continue to be so** troublesome **when they come in to supper."**

"Afraid!" she echoed scornfully, **" I** like **to get them** locked up."

I looked in blank astonishment upon the human **monster before me.**

"Are you in earnest?" I asked. " Do you mean **to say that you like to add to** the **hard lot of** those poor **creatures by that dreadful punishment of soli-** tary ? "

" Yes, **I'm sure I do ! "**

And **with a coarse laugh she turned** away.

I hoped she could **not** mean **it; but** all of her ac- tions, and all the reports that I heard of **her,** tended **to produce** the conviction **that she had formed a** just **estimate of her own character ;** and, **upon** that, made **a correct** representation of **herself.**

That **remark of mine hit wide of the mark.** Instead of touching her compassion it roused the spirit of mischief.

She was on duty that night in prison, and, restless as the renowned adventurer who went to and fro in the earth seeking whom he might devour, she went on a search through the cells of the first division where my kitchen women lodged.

The Deputy had ordered me to supply the women, on that division, with all the blankets they wanted, because they worked in the kitchens where it was hot and the air full of steam. And being the lowest tier of cells, they were colder than the others.

I had done as he directed me, so that some of them had four or five. Allen, my steam woman, an old woman of nearly sixty, had six.

Mrs. Hardhack stripped their beds, and counted their blankets. She took off all but two, and locked them up in a black cell.

The sweep who sat 'tending the door saw the proceeding, and ran to tell me what was going on.

"Mrs. Hardhack is stripping the blankets off the women's beds, and she hasn't left poor old Allen but two little strips of rags."

I went to see what she was doing. No sooner did her eye light on me than she commenced to show me how well educated she was in the use of the dictionary.

"Here are your women with six blankets, and the rule is that they shall have only two. A double one and a single one."

I was in no wise accountable to her, and did not think it necessary to answer. I stood and looked at her. She went on, —

"You have no right to give your women more than the rest have. You have no right to give out blankets in that way, and the Master will know it directly. Here are your women with six blankets, and my shop women with only two. It's a shame to treat your women so much better than you do mine."

When she had exhausted herself, I said, quietly, but loud enough for them all to hear, —

"Your shop women are just as well treated as my kitchen women. Some of the old ones have five or six blankets — they all have as many as they wish for. I have been to the doors, and asked every one of them if they wished for more. And now if any woman wants another blanket, speak! and she shall have it. You may be assured, every one of you, that you shall have every comfort, from me, that I am allowed to give you."

No one spoke. That time Mrs. Hardhack failed to stir up jealousy on the part of the shop women towards me; or create disturbance in the prison.

"I shall have it my own way about the blankets to-night," she said, and locked them in a black cell.

I did not like to come in contact with her, so I went for the Deputy, to settle the matter. He was out. I asked for the Master. I was told that I could not see him. He was indisposed. I could not get

access to him, and my women slept without their
blankets till nine o'clock, when Mrs. Hardhack left
the prison.   After she was gone I returned them the
blankets she had taken away.

The next morning she came to me to know who
unlocked the black cell door.

" When you have authority to inquire into my ac-
tions, I will render an account of them to you."

" You have no right to unlock a door after I lock
it."

" You have no further care of the prison after you
leave it at night, and the last order given is the one
to be obeyed.   I had a plenty of blankets up-stairs,
in a chest, to supply the ones you took away, if I had
chosen to use them."

I went to the Deputy in the morning, and he for-
bade her interference in such matters.

She indulged herself in one more exhibition of
her sweet temper with regard to the affair, and that
was to tell me that she had secured my women a few
hours of cool repose.

IX.

ONE night, when the women were coming into the prison, I observed great commotion and disturbance among them. I heard a confused, mixed up, talk about beds being taken out.

Two or three of the women stepped out of the ranks, and looked up into their rooms, to see if their beds were taken out of them. Among the number was a woman by the name of Callahan.

I had heard of her as being a desperate character; but she had behaved well in the prison.

She was a tall, stout woman, with a loud voice. After she had looked into her room, and seen that her bed was gone, she turned to me, and asked, —

"What was my bed taken out for?"

"I didn't know that it was out."

She looked steadily at me for a moment; then, lowered her voice, and asked, —

"Do you mean to say that you didn't know that my bed was out?"

"Yes, Callahan, I meant to say that I did not know your bed was taken out. Perhaps you are mistaken, it may not be out."

"O, yes, it is out; I saw the naked bars."

"Come, Callahan, go along like a good woman! Go to your room first, and see, before you ask why it is done."

She went into her room. The other women were in theirs. I called, —

"Second Division!"

All of the rest shut their doors.

"Shut your door, Callahan!" I called pleasantly.

"No, ma'am, I will not. I don't mean anything against you; but I will not shut my door, nor sleep on the bars. Do you know who reported me, and what my bed is taken out for?"

"No, I do not."

I was obliged to leave her standing in her door, and go round to the other side of the prison to see the other prisoners slid in.

The moment I left Callahan, she began to rave. "By the Holy Jesus, I won't sleep on the bars. And I'll know who reported me, and what I'm reported for, — the miserable set of" —   .

"Callahan, stop!" I ran round and called.

Neither of the Shop Matrons appeared, and I was told that it was because they were afraid of Callahan's violence.

"No, I won't stop! I'll do something to make them lock me up. I won't sleep on the bars. It was Hardhack that reported me. I wish I'd struck her down!"

"No! no! it was Thingsly," said a voice that I did not know.

"Hardhack made the balls if Thingsly fried 'em. She's at the bottom of all the deviltry there is done here."

Then she commenced a tirade of vituperations and oaths that made my ears tingle.

In a few moments the Deputy made his appearance.

"Your No. 1 key," he said to me, and proceeded to Callahan's room.

I got it; and then followed him.

"Now, Mr. Deputy," she said to him, when he went up to her; "you know I won't sleep on the bars. You might as well lock me up first as last, if you are going to punish me. But you ought to tell me what it's for. I haven't done anything but speak in the walk, and all of 'em do that."

The Deputy made no reply; but I saw that he had buttoned up his coat as though he expected violence. She went peaceably to her solitary cell, however; but all of the way she begged the Deputy to tell her what he was locking her up for.

When she saw me standing by the Deputy, she asked me where Hardhack and Thingsly were.

"I don't know; they haven't been in the prison to-night."

"They're afraid to come; but I wouldn't hurt the poor little lambs. They know they're guilty, and they know I'm locked up for nothing."

"Shall I give her her bread and water to-night?" I asked the Deputy, as he turned to leave.

" Yes."

I knew the water would be grateful to the poor thing.

I wished to ask the Deputy if Callahan had told the truth; but my own consciousness told me that she had. I had learned to esteem the man, and I could not bear to hear him say that he was accessory to such injustice, although I knew that it was his duty as a subordinate officer to do as he had done.

I could not help questioning, Ought not the girl to be told what she is punished for? Has she been " admonished?" The poor thing had no redress for such injustice.

That was the point that she, too, was revolving in her mind. When I gave her the bread and water, she said to me, —

" Look here, now, don't you think they ought to tell me what I am punished for ? "

" You must not ask me such questions. It isn't for me to sit in judgment upon what the Master does."

She was intent on finding out my opinions, so she put her questions in a different way.

" If you reported me, wouldn't you tell me what it was for ? "

" Certainly ! I should probably give you a good scolding before I had you punished."

" If you was going to punish me just as you were a mind to, for speaking on the walk, would you shut me up here two days and two nights for it ? "

" Perhaps not ; but how do you know that you are to stay here two days and two nights ? "

" Because they are never shut up for any shorter time."

" O'Brien and McMullins were only in for one day and a night."

" That was because you begged 'em off. But nobody'll beg me off. Say! would you shut me up here for speaking on the walk ? "

" Perhaps not; but you knew the rule, and disobeyed, — it is for disobedience that you are punished."

" Ever so many of them talked, — they all talk ; but none of 'em got punished but me. They've got a spite against me, — is that right."

" Perhaps that is your jealousy, Callahan."

" No, it isn't. Four of us were talking together. If Thingsly saw one, she saw the whole of us."

" Perhaps it isn't for that you are punished."

" Won't you find out ? Won't you ask Hardhack ? "

" No, I don't wish to."

" Are you afraid of her ? "

" No ! "

" Do you like that woman ? "

" She is nothing to me. But if I were to ask her a question, about what does not concern me, I might not get a civil answer."

I was fast arriving to the conclusion that it would be impossible for me to assist in carrying out such a system of government.

The next day I spoke to the Deputy about letting her out. He shook his head.

"If she was one of your women, and you had the care of her, I might."

When the two days were expired, he sent me round word to let Callahan out at six o'clock. With my watch in my hand I did not defer it a moment later. As I was waiting upon her to her room, I asked her, —

"Why had you rather go into solitary than sleep on the bars?"

"If I sleep on the bars, I lose just as much time, and have to work all the next day. If I can't have my bed to sleep in, I won't work for 'em."

"I shouldn't think there would be much rest in solitary."

"There ain't; but I don't earn any money for them either."

There was retaliation with calculation.

"Callahan, I turned the key on you in solitary, and kept you there, — why are you not angry with me?"

"You didn't do it out of spite — you never did me any wrong. If they only punished me when I deserved it, I shouldn't be mad."

I did not know how to reprove the woman. "Callahan, be as good a woman in the shop as you are with me."

"I'll try to ; but they wake up the devil in me. I wish you would get me into the kitchen."

"I'll try."

X.

AN ARRIVAL.

THE windows of the kitchen were of ground glass. They were made to let down at the top, but could not be raised at the bottom.

When they were let down, I noticed that the younger women, if I were out of the way a moment, sprang upon the window-seat, which was a deep recess, and stood looking out. I inferred from the manner of doing it, and the apprehensive look they gave me, when detected, that it was breaking the rules to do so.

But no one informed me of such a rule, and I did not think it necessary to inquire. I could see no possible harm that could come to them from looking through the bars upon the grass, and trees, and flowers of the grounds. Positive good might arise from changing the tenor of their thoughts. If they stood longer than I thought best, I sent them to do something for me.

One day, Annie O'Brien had mounted the window-seat, in my absence from the kitchen, and when I went back, was exercising her powers of description upon what she saw, for the entertainment of the others.

The window through which she was looking, commanded a view of the yard, the office, and the walk through which the public found entrance to the buildings.

"An arrival, an arrival!" called Annie, in a loud whisper.

"Who is it? Is it anybody that we know?" asked one of the girls that had been brought in with her.

I stood behind the furnace a moment to notice what was going on.

"Yes, there is Tom Ticket. I wonder what he has been doing."

"Nothing new, of course! They wanted a carpenter down here, so they sent up for him. The carpenter was discharged the other day, and I heard one of the men say they'd have another down in a few days, — they knew just where to lay their hands on one of the best in the city."

"Do you mean to say, Lissett, that they can have a man brought down here a prisoner, because they want a carpenter?" I asked.

"Yes, ma'am. They know he drinks, and can prove it, but they don't want too many at a time, so they let him run till they want him; then, they have him taken up, and fetched down here."

My face must have expressed the utter abhorrence I felt of such work. O let us cleanse our whited sepulchres! Is there not work enough within our own borders to employ our Christian men and reforming women! We need not go abroad for work

with such festering sores in our own vitals. For
very shame let us cleanse these places ! — were my
thoughts.

Here was another occasion for glib Annie O'Brien
to hold forth ; and such occasions were never slighted
by her.

"Half that come in here," she said, "are not doing
anything when they come. My coming, when I
came, was a put up job."

"What do you mean by that?"

"A policeman was hired to take me up. I was
sitting in a store, about nine o'clock in the evening,
when he came in and told me to follow him."

"Who put him up to it?"

"A man that kept a saloon paid him five dollars,
and he did it. Any of the policemen will take a
person up for five dollars. When I came here I
wasn't doing anything out of the way ; but, of course,
they knew what I had done."

"What did the saloon man want you taken up
for?"

"Because I wouldn't tend for him. He had tried
to get me in there, and I wouldn't go."

"Why wouldn't you go? Wouldn't it have been
better for you to earn an honest living?"

"An honest living! I'd had to gone with any man
he said if I'd gone there, and I rather choose my own
friends."

"O, Annie, how can you stand there, and tell this
over? I should think your heart would burst with
grief when you think of it!"

" O pshaw ! it's nothing when you get used to it ! " said Lissett, and snapping her fingers at the imagination that O'Brien had called up, she flounced out of the room. But for all that, I saw that she choked as she said it, and the tears came in her eyes.

" I hadn't got quite so used to it as to go to that pitch," said O'Brien.

And where are the men that make these women what they are ? I asked myself. Coolly walking the streets outside the terrors of the law. At that moment I could have locked all of mankind in solitary, and fed them on bread and water, without suffering one pang. Is there no help for this state of things, that the weak suffer for the sins of the strong ? If man does not meet his punishment here he is borne on, by time, to judgment, where he will have no power to screen his guilty acts or shift his punishment upon the helpless.

That reflection did not satisfy me at the time. A more summary retribution would be better suited to the sin. One that would inflict immediate tribulation and anguish upon him, such as had fallen upon his victims.

Annie turned again to look out of the window.

" There is but one woman taking a ride in the fancy carriage of the government. Exercise in that carriage is excellent for dyspepsia."

" Do you know her ? " asked Allen.

" No ! she's a jail-bird, I know, by her looks. She's come from the Superior Court ; she'll have a long sentence. She's coming through the kitchen."

Annie sprang down to look at her, and all of the rest followed her to the door which stood open, into the garden, for the men to bring in the bread for supper.

"Stand back! It isn't necessary for you to give her a welcome."

The newly arrived had her veil drawn tightly down over her face; but I could see that she was young, and very good looking.

In the absence of the female Receiving Officer I took her from the Clerk, and waited upon her to the reception room where she was stripped of her own clothes, and put into a bathing-tub. When she was thoroughly scrubbed and dried, she was arrayed in the uniform of the place, and sent to the shop.

There her capabilities were tried, and she was assigned to the work for which she was best adapted.

The clothes that she had taken off were carefully folded, put in a bag by themselves, and labeled, to restore to her when she went out of the prison.

When I returned to the kitchen, my girls had found out who the new prisoner was, how long a sentence she had, and what was the offense for which she had been committed.

How the facts got circulation in so short a time, was a mystery to me.

7

XI.

In deciding upon the capabilities of the prisoners Mrs. Supervisor made herself useful.

Her first care was to find out how long a sentence a woman had. That determined one qualification for her own service. If the sentence were for two or three years, and there was to be a vacancy in her own family, the woman was eligible to a place there, provided she could be trained into the work required.

This care was taken to save herself and her House-keeper the trouble of changing.

To oversee her housekeeping was the Supervisor's pet employment, and it was fortunate for the House-keeper that the government super-official had one pet. Through that partiality, she got two hours and a half more sleep in the morning than the rest of us.

She was not called till half past six; but I un-locked her women at the same time that I did the others.

I was glad she could be so favored; but I could not see the justice of such an arrangement.

I found, in the course of time, that it was a system of mutual favor. I went in to breakfast one morning, and there was no milk on the table.

Katie, the table girl, went to the refrigerator, that stood in the room, to get me some. She had just laid her hand upon the bowl when the Housekeeper, with a quick motion, arrested her.

" I must have that cream for the Master's breakfast ! " she whispered.

She took the bowl, removed the cream into one pitcher, poured the skimmed milk into the one Katie held in her hand, and sent it to me.

I was not particularly anxious to drink skimmed milk in my tea so that the Master might have cream ; but I supposed it was in some way to contribute to the support of the institution ; or that there was an order of the Board to that effect, so I made no complaint. Indeed it was my policy not to appear to notice what was going on in such trifling matters, — trifling to the Supervisor, probably, whatever they might have been to the inferior officers.

Before I knew the Housekeeper's hour of rising, I went into her kitchen, on an errand, several times before she was up.

I always found the women working on nice embroidery. They could not attend to their housework because the Housekeeper had the keys, and was not up to unlock the stores and give out the things to work with. But there could be no relaxation of their labor on that account. They must be up and at work.

One morning, Mary Hartwell asked me to look on the list, and see if her name were there.

The names of the women who were going out during the month, with the date of the day that they
were to be discharged, was handed to the Receiving
Matron, the first of the month.

The women were very accurate, usually, in keep-
ing account of their own time, still they were anxious
to have their own calculations confirmed by knowing
that their names were entered on the discharge list.

"If you will please look for me, I will do something for you after I go out."

" Something for me, Mary! O no! I will look for
you when I go to the wash-room to-day."

Her remark called my attention to her work. I
saw that she was doing a beautiful piece of embroidery. When she saw that I noticed it, she held it up
and exhibited it with a great deal of pride.

It was a night-gown yoke, in linen, of an elegant
and elaborate pattern.

" Who are you doing this for?" I asked.

" This is for Mrs. Means." That was the Housekeeper.

That is what I call you up two hours and a half
before she rises, to do, I thought.

" How many of you are there that can do such
work?" I asked.

" Five of us can do this kind, and we can all do
fine stitching, or crochet, or some kind of fine needle-
work."

There were ten of them to do the work in the
Housekeeper's rooms, and those of the Supervisor.
Quite an array of talent!

" You ought to see Ann Horton's work. She does all kinds beautifully. She stays up-stairs, and works all of the time. She had a sentence of three years; it's most out now. It would do your eyes good to see the piles and piles of nice things she has done for the Master's wife and the young ladies. The pillow-cases, and the yokes, and bands, and skirts."

" Has she been doing embroidery all of the time for three years ? "

" Yes, ma'am, and nice sewing."

I thought three years of hard labor, from five in the morning till eight at night, must accumulate quite an amount in value, of such work, beside what was done at intervals of two or three hours at a time, by the other nine women.

Supervisor might have exercised her thrift in supporting the institution, very profitably, by selling that embroidery as she proposed to do the moth-eaten rags. In doing that she might obviate the necessity of giving the officers skimmed milk in their tea.

I inferred that that three years' labor was a perquisite belonging to the office of Supervisor. In addition to her salary she was making a profitable affair of her sinecure situation. Far more advantage would accrue to her than to the institution in having such an incumbent.

Supervisor of what? Of her own housekeeping. The very best of employments for a woman if she has a family.

XII.

SUNDAY.

It was Sunday morning. Sunday was our busiest day, because our meals came so near together.

We were allowed one hour more of sleep on this morning than on the others. I had waked at the usual hour, but settled myself comfortably to rest again hoping to obtain it. Tinkle, tinkle, went the bell over my head. I paid no heed to it for a moment. Rattle, rattle, rattle went the noisy thing for full ten minutes. By that time, vexation had expelled all drowsiness.

I vowed, in my own mind, that I would muffle it the next Saturday night, in retaliation for the unseasonable summons. At first I determined to disregard the call. It must have rung from habit.

The next thought that suggested itself brought me to my feet. Perhaps a new order had been issued, and subjected to the approval of the Board at that early hour. In that case the august mandate was not to be disregarded. I rose, unlocked my women, and set them to work.

The ringing of the bell so early proved to be a mistake of the watchman, who was a new hand, who fearing he should be late, gave me that untimely warning. I judged, from that circumstance, that the orders were as distinctly given, and the duties as definitely arranged on the other side as on ours.

I grudged that hour of lost repose both for myself and my women. I was hungry for rest; and my women were worked to sheer exhaustion.

Sunday all of the women were unlocked at six o'clock. They were called out of their rooms, in the same order as on other days, left their skillet pans, and the quarts in which they had taken their suppers to their cells the night before, at the slide, as they went out. They were marched to the shop to wash and be dressed for chapel. While they were gone, their dishes were washed, and their breakfasts put into them to be taken to their rooms when they returned to them.

At nine they were marched to chapel, where they remained till half-past eleven or twelve, when they returned to take their dinners, and remain in their cells till half-past one. Then, they went to chapel again, and returned at three to take their suppers to their rooms, and be locked in.

After that the presence of only one Matron was required in the prison. One of the other three was required to remain on the premises. Two might go where they liked.

Sunday breakfast and supper was of bread, mush, and rye coffee, the same as other days. The dinner was of roast beef, which was cooked at the bakehouse, and sent in to us to be carved and served.

The gravy was to be made in the kitchen, and the potatoes steamed : the meat and potatoes put into the pans, and the gravy poured over them.

To get that meat to its right destination required sharp care on my part. There were extra women sent in from the wash-room to help on Sunday. They, with my own, were possessed with a disposition to get possession of the greater part of that rarity.

They got up all sorts of inventions to get me out of the room, while it was being sliced, in order to secrete a part of it for their own use, the next day, and for that of their favorites among the prisoners.

At first they had been able to impose upon my ignorance, but at this time I had learned just how much two hundred and eighty pounds of meat would divide to about four hundred people. I had learned their " tricks and their manners " also, so that it had become impossible for them to draw me from my object, which was, to see it equally divided.

" An' sure ma'am," said Bridget O'Halloran ; " we're wanting the pails from the hospital."

In order to get the pails I must go to the outside door, blow my whistle to call a runner, wait till he came, and then order my pails. The hint was just in season. Allen had taken the first piece on her fork to commence carving. I said to her, —

" Don't cut that meat till I come back, not one slice."

I then ordered in the pails, and bread — every-thing that would be wanted before dinner, and took

my station at the table with the determination not to
be drawn away from it upon any pretense.

The smell of the meat to the poor, half-fed things
was very savory, and they came around picking up
the bits which fell off while it was being carved.

" Please ma'am, give me a bone, — just the least
bit of bone!" was the cry perpetually in my ears.
And the bones I was forced to give to their impor-
tunity as fast as they were freed from the meat.

To keep their fingers from that meat was like
fighting eagles from a dead carcass.

Bridget O'Halloran's ways were suspicious. I
thought she had eluded my vigilance, and secreted
some of it in spite of me. I kept watch of her mo-
tions for the rest of the day.

I noticed that she visited the shed very frequently.
If I wanted her I was continually obliged to send for
her. At last I thought I would go myself and see
what attraction that old shed had become so sud-
denly possessed of.

When I discovered her she was stooping down in
the middle of the building without any apparent object in view.

" Bridget — I want you in the kitchen at this
moment!"

She was fumbling about her stocking. I stood
looking at her while she was apparently arranging it.

" What is the matter with your stocking, Bridget?"

" Nothing, ma'am!"

She colored, was confused, and started with the top of it in her hand. I let her pass on before me so as to get a better prospect of what was going on.

From the glimpse that I got of her leg I thought she had been following the fashion — in adopting false calves. In hurrying her I had spoiled the proper adjustment of them, and they had slipped to her ankles. I intended to examine into the case when I reached the kitchen; but an explanation came by way of accident.

In order to make more speed, as I hurried her on before me, she let go the top of her stocking, the weight of what was in it brought it down over her shoe, and out fell two or three slices of meat. The cause of her clumsiness in moving was explained, also of her frequent absences. She had slily slipped away slice after slice, one at a time, and gone into the shed to secrete them in that safe place.

Under my eyes, as I stood looking at that meat, she had done it.

" Stop ! pick up your meat, Bridget ! "

" It's no matter, ma'am ! "

Her face was ablaze with disappointment and smothered anger, and tears filled her eyes.

" Stop, and pick up that meat ! "

She did so.

" Now look me in the face ! "

That was a hard command for her to fulfill; but she looked up at me.

" Caught in the act of stealing ! You do not in-

tend to treat me any better than you do any one
else?"

"I did not mean it against you,—indeed I
didn't!"

"Every rule that you disobey is something done
against me."

"I suppose you will report me; but I was awful
hungry."

"The rest of the prisoners are awful hungry;
you are no worse off than they when you share
equally with them; but if you rob them, in order to
help yourself to more than they have, you make
them worse off."

"I did not think of that. I work hard, and I
earn a good living, and I mean to get it if I could.
It's a shame for me to go hungry when I work so
hard."

"If you steal food here, Bridget, you steal it
from your fellow-prisoners, not from the institution. There is just so much allowed for you all, and
the rest won't get any more, in any way, if you take
it from them. They must go without if you have it;
and they work just as hard as you, and get no more
for it."

"It makes me awful mad to think I work so hard,
and don't get any pay for it."

"Then you ought not to come here. You have
been here before, and you knew just how it was before
you did the wrong which brought you here. You
were sent here to work hard, for nothing, for a punishment."

"Others do worse than I, and they don't come here. If those that put me here had their dues they'd be here too!"

That was the continual rejoinder.

"May be; but how are you going to help that? You will have about as much as you can do to attend to your own case. Only think of what you have been doing; robbing another person as badly off as you are. You ought to have pity on each other, if no else has pity on you! You ought to respect the rights of your fellow-prisoners, — they have done you no harm!"

"I will; but I was so hungry and the meat smelt so good; and I did not think of them. If you worked as I do, and was real hungry, and saw the meat, wouldn't you take it?"

"I don't know, Bridget; I have not had the temptation."

The word temptation sounded out from the other words that I had been using, fearfully loud when I pronounced it. A nice slice of roast beef was a strong temptation to those hungry women. They were allowed enough to tantalize but not to satisfy them.

By being kept without enough to satisfy their hunger they were led into sin, if it be a sin for them to help themselves to more than their share. They were led to disobey the rules, which involved punishment if they were detected. It would certainly undermine their health to work so many hours as they were obliged to without a suitable amount of food to produce recuperation.

"Are you hungry enough to eat that meat after it has been in your stocking, and on this floor?"

"Yes, ma'am; it ain't hurt it any. I'll eat it if you'll give it to me."

"Eat it!"

She brushed the dust off it with her hand, tore it apart with her fingers, and put it in her mouth.

"Bridget, don't ever take any more, and secrete it without my knowledge."

"No, ma'am; and you wont report me now."

"I gave you the meat. How can I report you?"

"Thank you!"

"If you are ever so hungry, don't you put any away for yourself without asking me!"

"No, ma'am!"

Perhaps she will not. The fear of punishment, in a solitary cell, had not deterred her from taking the meat. Perhaps pity for her fellow-prisoners would not; nor the desire to please me.

That evening I heard the Matrons discussing the music by the quartette choir in the chapel of the prison.

"You have a hired choir?" I asked.

"Yes, and an organ?"

That information sounded strangely in contrast with the scanty meals and the solitary cells.

Where does the praise of God come in?

XIII.

AFTER the kitchen was put in order, that Sunday afternoon, I gathered the women around me, and read a story to them, from a religious newspaper.

I also read them one of the Saviour's parables. Then, I talked with them so as to find out what ideas they entertained of themselves, and the lives they had led.

"What are you in here for, Sarah?" I asked of a smart, bright, active woman. As she was among convicts she was called bold; but if she were working outside she would be called a smart, capable woman. If any notice were taken of her ways she would be just remarked as independent.

"For shoplifting, ma'am;" and with a toss of her head, that was intended to ward off reproof, she added, "When I go out of here I will do just so again. I'll take five dollars for every day they've left me here."

"Then you will get detected, and brought back again."

"No, ma'am! I'll look out for that."

"You cannot; you may be sure your sin will find

you out. If you break God's commandment, 'Thou shalt not steal,' his eye is on you, He will see it, and surely punish you for it. It may be by coming here, and it may be in some other way."

"I'll risk all He'll do to me if I don't fall into the hands of the police, and get in here."

"That's my case," said Bridget. "The Lord knows just how poor we are, and how hard it is for us to get along; and He knows how the rich folks crowds on us, and He pities us. And He knows how they lie, and cheat, and steal from each other, — and He won't punish us any more nor He does them."

"It will make no difference to you what they do to each other, or what He does to them. You will not have to answer for their misconduct, nor be punished for it. You will only suffer for the commands which you break."

"We shall get into their company once where they can't put on airs over us; and that'll be a great comfort. I hope I shall be there when some of 'em go to judgment."

"If you are you may have enough to do to attend to your own affairs."

"If I was in the lower end of the d—l's kitchen, I shouldn't be too busy to see them sprinkled with brimstone."

"Hush, Bridget! that is revenge!"

"We can't help it," said the ever ready O'Brien. "I'd like to pay them back what they've done to me.

Don't you suppose we've got human feelings? Only think what that miserable Hardhack has made me suffer in solitary. Wouldn't I make her suffer back again? I'd beat her till she couldn't stand, the first time I meet her, if it wasn't for getting another sentence. One girl did give her an awful pommeling, and scratched her face; and she got another six months for it."

"O Annie, that is a bad temper!" but I thought I would study her still further. "I don't see why just the idea of being punished should make you so angry. I had you punished. What would tempt you to strike me?"

"Nothing on earth, ma'am! I would stand between you and a blow if it broke my head."

"But I had you locked in solitary."

"Yes, ma'am, and you was sorry for it, and I deserved it. But when they lock me up for nothing it makes me mad."

"Who is to be judge of when you deserve it? It would not do to leave it to you. You would never think you deserved it."

"You are mistaken there, ma'am. Didn't I tell you to report me when I was locked up? Didn't I say that I deserved it? You might have some of us locked up every day, if you were a mind to; but it wouldn't make us a bit better."

"It would make me very unhappy to do that. It would make me sick at heart to see you such bad women as that."

"We know it, and that keeps us from a great many things. But you might, for what we do, if you had a mind to, just to show your authority. You don't get mad, and we don't. You try to make us better, and we wouldn't any of us be mean enough to do wrong on purpose."

"I could not have you punished when I see that you are trying to do right. It is when you do wrong, and are determined to do wrong, that I shall have you punished. I see that you are improving in governing your temper, Annie. You don't get angry so easily as you used to, and you don't give way to it when you are angry, as you did two or three weeks ago."

"I don't think I do; but I should if you got mad and scolded me. If I do anything wrong, you turn round so calm, and talk to me so, it makes me ashamed; and I think of it when I want to do it again, and it keeps me from it, because I know you'd make me ashamed again. You have the upper hands of me. When I was in the shop, Hardhack would get mad and scold me, and that would make me mad, and I would sauce her; and then I got punished. If she hadn't got mad first I shouldn't."

It occurred to me that the officers of the institution would do well to study the rule of the Board which directs that "no irritating language" be used to the prisoners. The provision was a good one. It needed an additional quality, the oversight which compelled it to be carried out.

"If I were to get angry and scold I could hardly

8

have confidence to teach you to be gentle and good-tempered. Now, Sarah, as you are only here Sunday, let us talk about the crime that brought you into this place."

" It wasn't a crime, ma'am. I'm sure I only took from the rich. I never lifted from any but the big stores where they lie and steal and make fortunes. I never went into any of the little small places, where they are trying hard for a living. I wouldn't be guilty of such a mean thing."

" Honor among thieves," says the old proverb.

" But it did not belong to you, without regard to the way they got it. You gave nothing in return for it."

" It did not belong to them, either. It belonged to me as much as it did to them. It would be hard telling who the right owner is. I thought I might as well have my share."

" I do not see that you had any share in it. You were taking that for which you made no return to any one, and that was stealing."

" If it had belonged to them it would be stealing. They take it, and dress their children up, and make a great show on it. My children are as good as theirs. Don't you suppose I want them drest up as nice when they go to school, and look like other children? I can't earn the things if I work ever so hard, so I lift from those that cheat out of others."

" Do you see what examples you are setting them? You are bringing them up to be thieves; and instead of the fine things which you covet for them, they will be drest in the same uniform that you are."

"Never, ma'am; never! my children shall never be thieves!"

"But they will do as you do."

"No, ma'am, they will not do as I do. They shall not. They go to day-school, and to Sunday-school, and say their prayers at night. They will never do as their mother does!"

In saying that she choked down the sobs that rose in her throat, and brushed off the tears that were gathered in her eyes, just ready to run over the hardy old cheeks.

"If they grow up to think differently from what you do,—to look upon the sin of stealing as it really is,—they will be greatly grieved that you have committed such acts. They will be ashamed of the clothes you have stolen for them. Every time they look at them they will think, my mother stole this dress. They will think everybody knows that she stole it. They will be ashamed to look any one in the face. The other children will taunt them with it, and they will be miserable, and they will turn it back upon you. They will blush for their mother; then, how can they respect or love her!"

If there were a tender spot in that mother's heart I meant to probe it, and I succeeded. She covered her face with her hands, and her chest heaved. The big tears made their way through her fingers. She was determined to brave it out. In a very few moments she mastered her emotions, and answered me,—

"They don't know what I do, and they never shall know it."

"Don't they know where you are now?"

"No, ma'am!"

"Where do they think you are?"

"Gone a journey."

"You may deceive them that way for a time; but you are only adding sin to sin. God says ' the iniquities of the parents shall be visited upon the children.' You may be sure that they will know it in the end. It was put in the papers when you came here. It is imposible to conceal what you have done, and where your sin has brought you."

"I didn't come here in my own name."

"Every one in here knows your real name; so do all of your acquaintances outside. You cannot save your children the knowledge and disgrace of your crime. Then, consider what you suffer from it."

"I don't care what I suffer, if I can only get the things for them. Talking is one thing, and living another. My children shall look as well as the best of them they go with."

That one idea had been ground into her mind by the force of her associations — the one idea of dress. It was in those above, around, below her. She had adopted it unconsciously, irresistibly.

The mother's love and pride were in that woman's heart in all their strength, and they had been developed by the circumstances around her. She did not care what she suffered if they could only be supplied

with the good things which she valued because she
saw the whole world setting the high price upon
them. Body and soul might be the sacrifice ; no
matter, so she obtained them. Into what a strangely
perverted channel had that mother's love run. Was
that noblest, best of woman's instincts to destroy
that woman's human life, and ruin her soul? God
knows! He also knows how much of her sin rests
upon those who profess to be following after better
things ; but have set her the example to make the
obtaining of dress the business of her life ; and
placed the temptation in her way to do it dishon-
estly.

How much of the guilt he who causes his brother
to offend ought to bear, must be decided by the
Higher Judgment.

"If God had seen fit to gratify your pride, in your
children, He would have provided a way for you in
which you could have done it honestly. As he did
not, you ought to have submitted to your lot, and
done the best that you could."

How hollow those words sounded to me as they
came from my lips. How easy it is to preach sound
doctrine. How hard to make an impression, with it,
upon minds and hearts established in their own
opinions of right and wrong, and persistent in the
determination to follow the wrong! If I could have
had that woman under my influence a year, I might
have led her into different views and ways. She was
not wholly hardened, as her tears showed.

" God did intend that I should have it, and that was His way of giving it to me. He made me light-fingered, and gave me a chance to help myself. I'm willing to leave it to Him. I don't believe He will judge me any harder than He will those I took it from."

She fell back again upon what others do. I had made no progress in dispossessing her of the idea that the wrong of another mitigated her own.

" The command reads, ' *Thou* shalt not steal.' If the men that keep those large stores steal, you are not responsible for it. It is only for what you do that you will be called to give an account."

" Line upon line," I thought. " I hope you will never come in here again."

" I never mean to," and she nodded her head as much as to say, I'll be bright enough to avoid that.

" I hope you will never again do the things that brought you here."

" I shall, ma'am. For every day I'm in here, I'll have five dollars out of 'em."

She did not say this so vauntingly as she had made the assertion at first. Still there was the spirit of retaliation, of revenge, upon some one for her punishment.

" In doing that, who do you think you will spite ? "

She stopped to think a moment. The question had taken her at unawares.

" I don't know. Them that put me here."

" But if you go into their store, they will know you, and watch you, and you will get caught again."

" Then I'll have it out of some of the rest of them."

" How will that spite the ones that sent you here?"

" They're all alike. It won't make any difference which I take it from."

" They are not all alike, any more than you and I are alike because we, just now, happen to be in the same place. If you go out of here and steal again, you spite yourself, and the punishment for it will fall upon your own head, and on the heads of those poor children that you have brought into the world. Those poor little things that are bone of your bone, and flesh of your flesh. Does not the mother-heart melt within you in pity for those children when they come to find out that their mother is a thief? O Sarah, if you are not afraid of God's judgment, which is the most fearful thing that can overtake you, let your children be in your thoughts when you go to take what is not your own, and turn you from your wicked purpose."

" She tells ye the truth," said McMullins. " And only think of me! Here I am, the mither of five beautiful chilter as ye ever set eyes on. And me heart is sick after them. The lads are with the father, and the little girls are in the alms house. Only think what a mither I am! I have ruined me-self for life, and damned me soul to hell forever."

" I don't believe anything about a hell," said Lissett. But she moved uneasily on her seat. It was easy to shake off the terror at the end of her tongue;

but it was to be seen that she was haunted by a fear of it in a conscience not quite seared.

"Ind.ade, there is. The praist has always told me that, and I've got it already whin I think what a mither I've been. God pity! God pity me!" This she said amidst sobs and tears.

"What kind of a wife were you, McMullins?"

"I don't care so much for the old man, he used to bate me sometimes, and he says he'll never live wid me any more. The minister went to see him for me, and he told him I had disgraced him; that he was fond of me once, but I had disgraced him, and put the chilter in the almshouse, and he would live wid me no more. Do you think he will? Only think what a miserable wife I've been! God pity me!"

"What did you come in here for McMullins?"

"It was all for a gallon measure, and a pint of beer. I wint in a store, and there stood a gallon measure, and a pint of ale widin it. An' sure I drank the beer like a sinsible woman; but I didn't know what to do wid the gallon measure, and I carried it to a policeman, and told him to take it. An' sure he brought me wid it to the watch-house, and thin, to the court, an' sure they gave me a year. Wasn't it too bad to give me the making of a year in here for jist a pint of beer and a gallon measure? Wasn't it a long sintence for a pint of beer, and a gallon measure?"

"I think you must have had something before you took the pint of beer and the gallon measure?"

" An' sure I had; but it was on that I lost my sinses, and got me sintence."

" You have been here before, havn't you ? "

" An' sure I have."

" You were put here, probably, to keep you out of the way of temptation. If you were out you would, probably, take another pint of beer and gallon measure the first thing you did."

" I don't believe I could help it."

" I don't think you could."

I turned to one of the other women and asked : " What are you in here for, O'Sullivan ? "

" For a home," said the slide woman, sharply.

" You must have a curious taste to choose this for a home."

" I had no other. The man what's the father of my child told me to steal a dress, and get in here, and be taken care of. I stole the dress, and he informed on me, and I came here."

" Why didn't he take care of you himself, after bringing that trouble upon you ? "

" He couldn't. He give me all his earnings ; but couldn't get work enough to do it all."

" An' sure he's nothing but a miserable drunkard hisself," said McMullins.

" It don't become the likes of you to say much about it if he is ! " snapped back O'Sullivan.

A poor, old reprobate, from the wash-house, whose hair was once red, now gray, sat next.

" What are you here for, granny ? " I asked.

" An' sure they swore a theft on me.   I didn't de-
sarve it.   I lived with a German family on Rust
Street.   They missed a solid hundred dollars, and I
never saw it no more nor a child unborn.   But they
got the sintence of ten years on me."

" How long have you been here, granny ? "

" Since seven years last Christmas."

A long sentence, if it is the first one.   I was sure
it was not.   A long life full of transgressions of the
law stretched itself upon her past history.

" What are you here for, Nellie ? "   I asked a
girl not twenty.

" A handsome Balmoral skirt took my fancy, and
I'm here for it.   I took a sup of liquor, and I was as
rich as a Jew.   I thought the Balmoral and all that
I saw was mine."

" It is glorious to feel so rich ! " said Lissett.   " I
mean to get a sup of liquor before I get back into
the city."

" And be brought directly back here again."

" I shall have that one time on them."

" On yourself, you mean.   It is all on yourself.
The law does not suffer, nor do those who execute it,
for your being here."

It was evidently a new aspect of the subject that
they were the greatest sufferers for their misdoing.

" It plagues them, or they wouldn't put me here."

" It is not because you plague them; it is because that you injure others that you are put here."

The spirit of revenge, upon some one, for the punishment they were receiving, was the one that was uppermost in their minds. Revenge against those whom they had injured in the beginning; against those who made the laws, or the officials who executed them. Their idea of revenge was to commit the same deed again.

" Don't you all feel ashamed of what you have done," I asked, " when you think of it ? "

" Yes, we do, that's the truth," said Annie O'Brien. " But's of no use. Nobody will ever think anything of us again, after we have been in here, and its no use to try to do any better ; and we just do as, bad as we can."

" But the All-seeing Eye is watching you, and, if you try to do right, will help you along. And in the life to come, where all hearts are known, you will get your recompense. Then, if you are really trying to do right you will be thought of and loved."

" It is a great while to wait for that, and it is hard."

" I know it is hard; but it cannot be long. It may be that we go at any moment; and then, it is forever and forever."

" If we could only keep that in our minds — but we forget it."

" You cannot of yourself. But if you ask the Father of your spirit to take your thoughts under his control, He will, and help you to think."

Poor things ! They were ignorant of the way to control themselves. They had few to teach them in it, and none to help them in their personal efforts to overcome the evil dispositions so long indulged in.

That night, when I went into the hospital, for the closing inspection, the nurse was grumbling about the trouble one of the women had given her.

"Indeed, ma'am, this is the awfulest place a woman can get into!"

I thought I would give her a hint that it was her own misdoings that brought her there.

"What brought you in here, Mary?" I asked.

"I made my fingers too nimble with a man's pocket-book."

"You did! then you don't deserve a very good place, do you?"

"I have got my pay for it."

"How came you to do such a thing?"

"He left some money with me to keep, and I did keep it so as he couldn't get it again. He got drunk, and I thought perhaps he wouldn't remember it agin."

"Men don't forget their money so easily."

"So I found to my cost."

"What did you do with the money?"

"I spent it for things that I wanted."

"You will hardly try that again if you ever have the chance."

"No, ma'am! I could have earned the two hundred and eighty dollars that I took in half the time I have been here, and had my liberty too."

"You knew it was wrong when you took the money and used it?"

"Yes, ma'am; but I wanted the things, and the

money was in my hand to buy 'em. The things would be of use; and I knew that drunken fellow would waste it if he had it."

Another specimen of specious reasoning; nor is that kind of reasoning confined to convicts.

"It was not yours; you had no right to it, and that ought to have been sufficient for you. If he wasted it in drunkenness that was his sin, not yours. You could have restrained him through the laws that punish drunkenness. You could have told him how wrong he was doing, and set him a better example. Instead of that you stole, and he got drunk. You made yourself as bad as he."

"I did not think of that."

"I hope this has taught you a lesson that you will never forget, — one that will make you think. Before you had this punishment you had not the strength to resist the temptation to take the money. Now you will always remember what you have suffered here, and you will not be likely to do it again."

"No, ma'am, I don't think I shall. This is harder than working for a living outside, besides the rough handling we get. A poor living at that, and poorer clothes. And you officers don't fare much better. You get a little better feed, and a better bed, and a little pay; but not so much rest; and you are in as close confinement as we are."

"But we are not prisoners; we can go if we like."

"What do you stay here for; you don't seem fit for such work, and you might earn a great deal more outside, and not work so hard?"

I may be able to teach a few of you, poor things, to live right when you go outside, and that will be better to me than money."

" God bless you ! that is what we want. There is many a one of us would be glad to live right if we knew how."

" There are some that only grow harder for coming here, and do as bad again, and come back."

" O, yes ! they think they're prison birds, and there's nothing more for 'em in this world, and they don't care. Nobody likes to have such as we about 'em."

" But there are people that would help you to lead a better life, and earn an honest living, if you could find them."

" They might find us, but it is hard for us to find them."

That was a very true remark. Our prisons are prominent institutions in the land. It is easy for any one who is interested in the cause of humanity to find them ; but to get access to them is a more difficult undertaking, as many can testify who have attempted it. I leave them to tell their own tale, and let it bear its own testimony. It is easy to find the poor wretches who are compelled to take up their abode within them, and do them good if one wills.

What a page of life was revealed to me in that one day ! What a work is there here for you to do, O women of this broad land, for your fellow woman, if you will address yourselves to it !

XIV.

It required the exercise of a large share of physical courage to enter, and examine into the condition of the private apartments of my boarders.

I shrank away from the task in loathing. Low, narrow, confined, they were like the cages of wild animals.

The human odor of the occupants had penetrated the walls and made the air noisome. They were ventilated through the bars of the door, and an apperture of five or six inches in diameter in the inner wall of the cell; but being used for all purposes, they would have remained uncleansed had every care been taken.

I went to the door of one, and looked in. I shivered, dreaded to enter, turned away. I went along to another. It looked comparatively tidy. A little white cloth embroidered around the edge with gay-colored thread, was laid carefully over the box. I stood and looked in while I reasoned with myself to screw my courage to the sticking-point.

I put my head within the door, the bugs were crawling along the walls, and the white-wash was spotted with marks of the violent death which had befallen many of them the night before. Again I shrank back in disgust. I called the white-wash woman to come with her brush and cover up the filthy sight, if she could not cleanse the dirt away.

If the sight is so revolting, what must it be to sleep among them, to be lodged with, and fed upon by them. I worked up my feelings of pity for the poor prisoners till my disgust was partially overcome.

The rats and mice can come in at the open doors, and there is no obstacle to such ingress of bed-bugs. Indeed such armies of them as I beheld could hardly have made their entrance in any other way. There they were in swarms, and had planted their colonies upon the solid brick and mortar, granite and iron, industriously, as the busy bee prepares her dormitory.

There is no ill to which the flesh is heir which has not been endured by the flesh. What has been endured by one flesh may be by another. In this case under modifying circumstances. Truly I can bear the sight of these vermin, and attend to their destruction with much less suffering than those poor women can be made their prey night after night.

My indignation was aroused against those who had charge of this place, and who, in their neglect, had allowed these dens for the confinement of human beings to become breeding nests of vermin. That indignation gave me courage and energy for my task. I set one of my sweeps to the work of slaughter. I stood by and directed the cleansing with shivers of disgust creeping along my flesh, and thrills of indignation stirring my heart.

When the Deputy came round, I gave vent to my feelings in a side-thrust of sarcasm. I stated to him the condition in which I found the cells, and then asked, —

" Did these bed-bugs get a sentence here for life ; or did they come, a special beneficence to the prisoners, by an order approved by the Board ? "

" We have the beds taken down, and filled with new straw in the spring, and the cells white-washed, and the frames washed. It has just been done, you know."

" To what purpose you can see. It could not have been properly done. If it had they would not have recruited so quickly."

" I will give you a bed-bug woman, whose special business it shall be to look after and exterminate them."

" Some poor old cripple, I suppose, who would be an additional care. It is no matter about the woman."

I was vexed that the cells had been allowed to get into such a condition. " It is very disagreeable to make them clean. I can keep Berry at the work. If I do not keep her hands busy her tongue is hatching mischief. If I do not keep her at work I can't keep the track of her. She is over to the wash-house, down to the shop, or hospital, gossiping, and carrying news."

Berry was the white-wash woman. After the other two "sweeps," or prison chambermaids, had swept the cells, and walks, her work was to go around with her white-wash brush, and cover up any soil or stains which had been left upon them.

"Suit yourself. I will do all I can for you."

"Thank you! If I could have one smart, healthy woman in the kitchen, it would help me very much."

"O, a smart woman! we must have the smart women in the shop. We can't spare you a shop hand."

"I have enough that are maimed and halt, and blind, now."

"You know a greenback covers every bundle of contract work that is done in the shop," he said, with a knowing wink.

"And the women must be made to help support the institution. There may be various ways of doing that. Greenbacks may look very nice to you men; but will not the health and reformation of those woman be as much money in the treasury of the state as the greenbacks which cover that contract work?"

"That is the Master's order. He is bound up in that contract work. He knows just how much each woman does. He examines the tickets himself, every morning."

"Would you work the women in that way if you were Master here?"

"I am not."

" Just let me tell you what an able-bodied corps I have in the kitchen. Old Allen, the steam woman, has a broken wrist. The cook is lame in one of her hips. One of the sink women has fits ; the women say. the other is a ' poor weak thing.' One of the slide women is in that condition which some women, of the class that are here, find themselves without a lord, and always demands consideration. Another has just got up from her confinement. One of the sweeps is blind of one eye, and can't see with the other. The only able-bodied woman that I have complains that I put every hard thing upon her to do."

The Deputy laughed good humoredly at my description, and said, —

" I will see what I can do for you ; but I'm sure the Master will not be willing to spare you one of his shop hands."

To get a large amount of contract work done, and show the figures that were received for it, was the Master's way of recommending himself to the Board of Directors ; and it was what enabled him to keep his place.

It must be an apparent fact to the most shallow comprehension, that dollars and cents are essential to the welfare of humanity ; but there are various ways of calculating their benefit.

The " almighty dollar " enlarges and increases in value, as it is contemplated, and its advantages dwelt upon. In the same ratio does an appreciation of human suffering decrease as it becomes familiar to the observation. The Master had evidently been through the mental process in both directions. The dollar had grown till it covered the whole surface of human life; the suffering had diminished till it became a mere speck in the distant view which he took of it.

" Let me have Callahan ? " I proposed.

" I don't believe it would be best," and he shook his head wisely. " You would get along with her, and she would make you no trouble; but it wouldn't be a week before she would be in a broil with the other women, and I should be obliged to lock her up."

" When she was in here before, she was in the kitchen four months, without being locked up, wasn't she ? She gets locked up where she is now."

He saw that I was informed upon Callahan's past history. She did a great deal of work in the shop; the Master would not be willing to spare her. He knew that to transfer her to the kitchen would be to interfere with Mrs. Hardhack's plan of breaking her temper, and she would resist her removal. His influence was not strong enough to overcome that of the two combined. He shook his head, —

" I'm afraid I cannot, and I do not think it would be best." He understood how to make his refusal palatable. " I think you are getting along well. I have been intending to tell you that I am satisfied with your management. The kitchen is clean and quiet; and the meals are prompt, much more so than they were for a long time before you came. They are well cooked, too."

"Thank you! but my women are worked beyond endurance. It makes my heart ache to see those poor cripples lifting out tubs of swill that two men could scarce handle ; and bucketful after bucketful of that large, heavy coal from the cellar, with all of their other lifting and scrubbing."

" I'll see what can I do about sending you another woman. Do the best you can ! "

" I will certainly do that."

After he had gone out, O'Brien said to me, —

" The Deputy wouldn't be hard on us, if he could help it."

I did the best I could. I told them I was sorry to make them work so hard ; but I could not help it. I asked them to do things, when I could possibly do it, rather than give a command.

When I had time I gave them a reason, for an order, and however tired they might be, that was sure to secure ready and prompt acquiescence.

" You must get on more steam as quick as you can, because we are a little behind time with our dinner," was sure to set Allen's fire going at once.

If I came in, and found them sitting down, idly gossiping away the time before their work was done, I had only to say, —

" Now, girls, start round, and get your work done ; then, you can sit down and talk. A clean room is so much pleasanter than a dirty one to me, and I want my place to look the nicest of any one in the institution, and you wish me to have the credit of its being so. You like to have all of the visitors taken in to see the kitchen because it looks so nice."

They would put the work about very quickly. Scrub and dust, and make the old kitchen shine like a new one in a twinkling.

"They were keen enough to fathom character, and took no advantage of my manner. They were conciliated; but did not lose the restraint of authority. They knew it was there, and could be used if necessary.

They never gave me impertinence; nor refused to obey when an order came directly from me.

That inspection day was a literal washing of the great Master's feet; not with my tears of penitence, but with the bitter remnants of pride and anger subdued to patience? My work was even more humiliating. It was that of the dogs, at the temple gate, cleansing the sores of the vagrant Lazarus.

The prisoners were allowed the condiments of salt, pepper, and vinegar. Their boxes and bottles were filled every Thursday. That was to last till the next Thursday. If they were wasted, or extravagantly used, they were obliged to go without till the replenishing day came. To attend to that was one of the duties of the chambermaids.

I was obliged to look after it or they would scatter and waste their allowance, and then play off on me. They would call to me, —

"I want salt; there was none put in my box."

That would be done from pure mischief, to get the

sweeps a scolding. But I gave them little chance to carry out their mischief in that way. I had the answer ready, —

" It was put there. I have been in every room to-day and saw it there. If it is gone you have wasted it, and must go without."

" I haven't wasted it."

" Wasn't it your pepper and salt that was strewed on the shop-floor to-day ? "

That hint that I was after them, and knew what they were about, was sufficient. There were no more complaints made.

Every woman was obliged to make, and tie up, her own bed. The prison women swept the rooms every morning. That gave them an opportunity to secrete many a nice bit for their friends. Indeed my sweeps ran a regular underground bakery express from the Master's kitchen, and also from the prisoners'.

Many a nice biscuit and slice of cake went from the range to the cells, and bread from my table was provided against mush morning, and brown-bread breakfasts.

Onions were a favorite vegetable, but their telltale odor enabled me to detect them easily.

One evening, I passed a cell where they gave out unmistakable evidence of their presence. I called to one of the sweeps, —

" Ellen, the gardener has made a mistake! He has put the onions, for the soup to-morrow, in one of those cells. Won't you take them out, and put them in the cellar. If one of the other Matrons, or the Deputy, were to come in, they would smell them as plainly as I do, and they might think you put them there for some one to eat privately, and get you reported."

That hint was sufficient; I never smelt onions in the cells again.

The officers professed to take no report from one prisoner against another; but when they got angry with a prisoner, and wished to remove her from their department, they did not scuple to avail themselves of information obtained in that way. Berry, my white-washer, was an apt agent. Sly, artful, and treacherous, she pretended sympathy, and got possession of knowledge which was Mrs. Hardhack's principal clew to find out what was going on in the kitchen and prison.

The other women understood, and avoided her. That made her angry, and the more watchful and treacherous.

One day she found a biscuit from the officers' table in a cell. She reasoned that Flannagan must have put it there, because Flannagan and the girl in whose cell she found it were great friends. That morning the Housekeeper had been fretted with Flannagan, and Berry had got wind of it. Here was the opportunity to exercise her vocation. She slipped the biscuit under her apron, took it into the officers' kitchen, and showed it to the Housekeeper.

Flannagan must have done it, because she had

given offense in the morning ; and she was forthwith dismissed to the shop.

A woman who came in a few days before, on a long sentence, had been discovered to be a nice needle-woman, smart and pretty ; whereas Flannagan was plain and slow. Occasion was thus made to effect the change, so my women said. And what they failed to find out in that institution was beyond investigation.

XV.

A DAY OF ODDS AND ENDS.

THE day commenced at odds. In the morning Mrs. Hardhack came flying into the kitchen, and demanded, from O'Brien, something for one of her girls to eat.

"She has fainted away for the want of food! She has had no breakfast! How did you dare to keep her breakfast from her!"

O'Brien kept her temper wonderfully. She answered very quietly, —

"I'm sure she had the same as the rest if she had been a mind to taken it."

"How do you dare to stand there and answer me in that way? I'll have you punished if you dare to open your mouth again."

O'Brien's face grew red, she opened her lips to retort just as I arrived to where they stood. I stepped between them.

"O'Brien, will you get a bucket of coal? I want more steam as soon as I can have it."

"Yes, ma'am," and she started away; but she looked up at me as she went as much to say, you have saved me.

I turned to Mrs. Hardback.

" I'm sorry one of your girls couldn't eat her breakfast; you know it is impossible for me to get anything aside from the Master's orders, and what the rest have. I'll see if I can find her something."

" We have got so much contract work to get done to-night, and, if the women faint away, they can't do it."

" I should be glad to provide them a good, substantial breakfast to work on ; but I can't have my way about it. It is very cruel to feed them as they are fed here ; and then, to work them as they are worked."

I thought, as I went to look up something for her to take to the poor girl, of the remark John Randolph made to his lady neighbor, when he entered her house and found her at work for the Greeks, " The Greeks are at your door." He had entered the house though a little army of naked, ignorant servants.

Do not the ladies of the United States need to be reminded that the Greeks are at their door? Are they not in every prison in the land ?

I went into the pantry. There was a skillet pan standing on the shelf with a bone in it. I took it out and inquired, —

" Whose bone is this ? "

" It is mine," said Lissett."

" Will you give it to the woman in the shop who fainted this morning because she had no breakfast ? "

" Yes, ma'am ! "

" Bring a slice of bread, and quart of coffee to go with it."

Handing it to Mrs. Hardhack, I dispatched her as quickly as possible. I was glad when she departed. Her visits to the kitchen were very disagreeable. She always managed to use the " irritating language," forbidden by the Board in their " Rules and Regulations," which stirred up the angry feelings of my women, and it took time and argument to get them settled down into calmness and quiet again.

" If it hadn't been for you, I should have been in solitary again," said O'Brien, after she left. " How I hate that woman ! "

" And so do I, and so do I ! " was echoed round the room.

" If you hate such ways never copy them ! "

" What's the use in scolding us ! She knows we can't help the victuals. If she wants to scold anybody she'd better scold the Master."

" He'd sauce her back again ; and then, both of 'em would get locked up. Wouldn't you like to see 'em both locked up ? " said Lissett.

" Yes, that I should ! " was echoed all around.

" I'd like to cut the bread for 'em," said O'Brien. " The slices would be thin."

" I would draw small quarts of water," said Lissett.

" Hush, girls ! Don't you know that you are now indulging in the very temper that looks so hateful to you when you see it in others."

Scarcely was I relieved of Mrs. Hardhack's anti-benign influence, when the Receiving Matron made her appearance, and asked, although in a very different manner, —

"Why didn't the women bring over their clothes?"

"What clothes?"

"Their sheets to be washed. This is their day. They take them from their beds when they get up, and carry them to the wash-house as they go down to the shop. My women, and the four who were sent up from the shop to help them, have lost an hour by the delay. I don't mind about mine; but the shop women will be late back; and then, I shall be complained of that I did not drive them hard enough, and get the work out of them sooner."

"I didn't know anything about it. If you had told me last night I would have attended to it. Some of the women asked me if they should take out their sheets; but I didn't know what they meant, and told them I would see. I will send the sweeps to gather them up immediately, and send them over."

"I forgot to tell you last night. They won't blame you but me; there is the trouble. I hate to have the Master come around, and find fault."

"Are you afraid of him?"

"No! I'm not a prisoner; but I always feel uncomfortable where he is, don't you?"

"I have only seen him once or twice; and then I

was very much inclined to laugh at the pompous airs he put on ; but a sense of propriety restrained me."

" I had a great deal rather not see him, especially, when he comes to find fault."

" He ought not to find fault with you in this instance. You are under no obligation to teach me the duties of my department. If you attend to the work in your own you do your duty."

" I know that. but I can't help myself. He says I am here to do whatever he orders me, and that I must do it if I stay. I am a widow, and have a boy to support, so I try to do all I can."

" He knows that ? "

" Yes, they all know it."

" And he takes advantage of it to compel you to do his wife's work while he gets the pay for it."

" That is the plain English of the whole thing."

" But you can get more pay outside for less work than you do here."

" Perhaps so, if I knew how to find it ; but I never have been so fortunate as to find it before."

I had gone out into the prison as I was talking with her, and stood at the door a moment after she had passed out ; but there was no chance for rest during my watch. There came the sound of scolding and contention after me, and recalled me to the kitchen. I hurried back. The fear that some of them would get into a quarrel, beyond my reach to control, always haunted me.

" What is the matter?" I called out at the door.

" The cook is so slow we shall never get this swill out, and I am trying to hurry her," said the sink woman. " She hinders me so I shall never get my work done."

" I can't do no faster than I can," called back the sink woman. " It is no use hurrying me."

" Stop! both of you! Lissett, you know Jennie is slow, and you must have patience with her. Do I not have patience with you? You only make matters worse by fretting. Jennie, you are slow. When you carry swill with Lissett, go as fast as you can, so as not to hinder her ; then rest when you get through."

" Do come along !" fretted Lissett, " You are enough to fret a saint."

" That can't be you, Lissett. Haven't I told you, many a time, that you ought to help each other along, instead of scolding and fretting at each other."

" It is hard work to drag her, and the swill tub too."

" Then go a little slower, and give her a chance to do her part. There is one thing that I wish to do myself, and that is the scolding, and I don't wish to have you take it out of my hands."

" If you do it all there won't get much of it done."

" There will be enough. I do not need help. And I can suit myself much better in doing it than any one else can suit me. In future, Lissett, you and Annie O'Brien will carry the swill together.

Then you can both work as fast as you please. Jennie, you and Allen may carry together; you can be as slow as you please. I wish to hear no more trouble over the swill."

I intended to arrange their work so as to avoid all collision ; but I sometimes failed. When I had put those, whom I thought to be the best of friends, at work together, some little difference would arise and separate them.

Directly I had a call in the prison. Berry could not get on with her white-washing, because Maggie had not done her sweeping, and came to me with a complaint, —

" Maggie won't sweep, and that keeps me waiting. Won't you tell her to sweep so I can white-wash ? "

" Maggie, why don't you sweep so that Berry can white-wash ? "

" I am, ma'am, as fast as I can. I have got all of the rooms to do before I do the floor."

" You need not wait, Berry. Take a broom and help her."

That was something that Berry did not calculate upon.

" If Maggie would get up in season she could get her work done herself; she loves her bed too well."

" I have told you of a way to get your work done if you do not wish to wait."

" You favor Maggie too much, and the other Matrons all say so. You ought to get her up in the morning, they all say."

" Take a broom and sweep that platform! Don't bring any tales to me from the other Matrons! When I wish you to teach me how to treat the women, I will ask you."

Berry chose to consider herself a very much injured woman, and began to snivel and grumble.

" I am going down to the shop to work. Maggie is so saucy I can't get along with her." She dared not express her disaffection towards me.

" Well, Berry, when you find yourself so much your own mistress as to go where you please, I will give you ' a character,' and you may go to the shop to work."

" What kind of a character? " asked O'Brien, who happened along at that moment.

" A good one. You are a pretty good woman, Berry. There is one fault which I think might be corrected by going to the shop. You are very much disposed to tattle, and that sometimes makes mischief. If you go to the shop, where you are not allowed to speak at all, you can't do that kind of mischief. That would save me, if it did not yourself, a great deal of trouble."

I heard no more about going to the shop.

The kitchen was quiet after dinner and the work, before supper, done. I threw my head back, in the large chair in which I was resting, and drowsed.

The women sat buzzing, on low stools, just behind me. I had been too sleepy to notice what they

10

were saying; finally a word or two that I heard attracted me to listen.

"Was you here, O'Brien?" asked Maggie; "when Ida Jones was pulled into the hospital by the hair of her head ? "

" Yes, I was, and I saw it with my two eyes. The Master pulled her by the hair of her head, and kicked her as he went along the walk ; and she a poor, half-witted thing too. That was six weeks ago, and she has been in the hospital ever since."

I was wide awake — thoroughly aroused when that story was completed.

"Maggie Murray, do you mean to say that you saw the Master pull Ida Jones along the walk, by the hair of her head, and kick her as he pulled her? You ought to be very careful how you tell such stories, unless they are true."

" It is the truth, ma'am !" said several of them in a breath.

" He took her by her pug, like this," and she took hold of the coil of hair on the back of O'Brien's head, "and dragged her along. We all saw it, and the Housekeeper saw it, and she said he ought to be reported to the Board. And that Matron, that skinny person, I forget her name, that was here, she saw it. There were a plenty that saw it. When you go down to the hospital, you can ask Ida what is the matter, and she will tell you so too."

" What did he do it for?"

" She said she was dead with work — she could

not sit at it another minute — she was ready to fall; and Hardhack reported her; and the Master was so mad, — some of 'em said so drunk, — he dragged her himself out of the shop, all of the way to the Hospital."

My face must have expressed the horror that I felt.

"Indeed it is the truth, ma'am!" said O'Brien. "The Master was crazy to get a lot of work done that night, and it made him awful mad to lose a hand."

I asked myself if it were possible that that man would dare to abuse the trust reposed in him in that manner. Certainly! The whole system of secrecy upon which our prisons are managed is just calculated to screen such conduct, and to induce the practice of it, if there be a tendency, in the disposition of the man who has charge, to do it. If the testimony of prisoners is not to be relied upon, a Master could make it for the interest of his officers to remain silent. Some might look at it in the same light that he did, and feel perfectly satisfied.

Why should not a prisoner's testimony be taken in a matter where he is concerned? He has been tried and convicted of an offense. Is that fact a conviction in every other case where he may have difficulty with another person?

If prisoners are entirely unworthy of trust, how does it happen that such a man, once a convict himself, according to the traditions of that prison, has charge there, and the unlimited confidence of the Board?

I noticed, in making out the report of inmates, that there were not so many women as men in prison. There was satisfaction in obtaining that fact, because I had entertained the idea that women were more frequently punished for their offenses than men.

It was a mistake, except in the one crime of licentiousness. In that man goes comparatively free, and woman is the only sufferer in what is, to say the least, their mutual sin. I say, almost every woman will say, and with truth, for the sin that man leads her into.

Woman does not seek man, in that way, in the first instance. He draws her into the sin, and when she becomes abandoned, and the Penitentiary brings her up, she is no worse than he. She becomes a night-walker, and suffers for her violation of law. He is a night-walker also, as miserable and degraded a man as she is woman; but who prosecutes him, and gives him a sentence in the House of Correction! He continues a night-walker unmolested while she suffers for her sin.

He walks into the parlors of the intellectually cultivated, and socially refined, — I was about to say virtuous woman. There can be little virtue in such shaky morality. I can only say of the chaste woman, and she takes the hand of the night-walker, and greets him cordially, and makes him welcome, especially if he be rich, — the hand that leads her fellow woman to her social ruin if not to her eternal death.

If woman were to help make the laws, could she remedy this state of things, — would she? Would she take her husband, father, brother from his home to the Penitentiary? She must do that, in order to rid society of the pest of night-walking. She may do that now if she will. The law gives her the opportunity. Instead of lavishing her courtesies, as she now does, upon the male offender, she might extend her charity in kindly assistance to his victim, if she were disposed to do it.

To judge by the way she treats him now, if she were to assist in making laws would she not be still more unjust than she now is, to her own sex, and lenient to the other.

If man go unpunished, of human law, for this sin, justice will find him out sooner or later. God pity him when his retribution comes! The avenging of a guilty conscience will work him greater woe than the miseries of a prison can inflict.

As I sat in the prison this evening reviewing my day's work, I counted up my occupations.

I am Housekeeper, Engineer, Overseer, Jailer, Porter, Usher, Sentinel, and many others which I did not enumerate.

Irksome as was the handling of keys to me, it was quite an entertainment to see myself answering the knock of the gentlemen in striped uniform, letting them into my kitchen, and following them around, like a page after a prince; and then, letting them out. I hardly think they get such attendances in the outside world.

Rotation in duties, and reversion in offices was the order of the place. I was Usher to the prisoners; my sweeps were stationed on the stone stairs, when the prisoners were in their cells, and the kitchen door locked, to open it if there were a knock on the outside, and to lock it again after the officer who entered.

Sittings on the stone stairs could hardly have been comfortable accommodations. I was reminded of that fact this evening, by hearing Ellen whisper when she heard a knock, —

" I hate to get up, — I've just got my seat warm."

" Every back is fitted to its burden," is an old proverb. I wondered if those prisoners had been provided by a beneficent Providence, of some kind, with an extra amount of animal heat, in order to warm up the stones they lived on during their incarceration.

XVI.

A FRIGHT.

SUPERNUMERARY was in the habit of sending to me for my No. 5 key occasionally. She said it let her through from the house into the attic of the prison.

I could not imagine what she wished to go through there for. I finally settled down upon the supposition that she wished to supervise the prisoners' rooms at her convenience, and see if I kept them in order, and made the poor things as comfortable as possible.

The mystery was unraveled when she took me up to show me the room of the Receiving Officer which she wished to have cleaned. She pointed to a large closet on the same flat, where she packed away summer articles of use in the fall, and winter ones in the spring, which she said my 5 key locked.

I had given her the credit of one generous deed too many. Still, although she went through on her own business she did have an eye to cast about upon the affairs of the prison.

One night, about eight o'clock, after she had been using this key in the afternoon, I was on the third flight of stairs. The Deputy went rushing past me, in great perturbation, looking deathly pale.

" What is the matter, sir ? pray what is the matter ? " I asked, as I turned back to follow him.

" Mrs. Martin says she heard some one in solitary,
this afternoon, in one of the upper cells ; and there
has been no one put in for three days."

" And I have fed no one up there for three days ! "
I exclaimed in an agony of apprehension. The
second thought followed fast upon the first. " It
cannot be, Mr. Deputy ! I have passed those doors
several times a day, and the sweeps sleep next to the
black cells. No woman would stay there three days
and nights without letting it be known. If there had
been any one there I should not have forgotten her,
and I don't think you would."

" Mrs. Martin says she heard her talk and sing
this afternoon."

" It cannot be ! She has been very cool to make
no mention of it till now."

But the thought of my having left any one so
long in solitary, without food, took my strength from
me. My limbs trembled ; I sunk upon the steps.

" It cannot be, Mr. Deputy, that we have been so
careless ! Mrs. Martin has been very cool about it.
She had my key about three ; it is now after eight.
No woman who had been in solitary three days without food would be merry enough to sing."

He slackened his pace ; but still said, —

" I am going to see ! "

When he came down I asked him what he found.

" An empty cell," he said quietly.

Mrs. Hardhack did not let her superior officer off so easily.

" I wish that woman could ever exercise a little common sense ! " was her gentle comment.

" She is Head Matron of this institution, — you ought to speak of your superiors with respect ; " was my sarcastic rejoinder. I could not choke down the remark.

The Deputy showed his humanity by looking into the matter as soon as it was told him, as much as such testimony, in his favor, is to the disadvantage of the brilliant and energetic Head of the female department of the prison.

That man was very acute in his management to get along pleasantly with the officers ; and obtain from them what service he wished. If he exacted labor of us, that he had no right to ask, he made the exaction tolerable by his manner.

One day we were without a Receiving Matron. On that day I had had the promise of having my kitchen white-washed, and had made my arrangements for it, so as to make it as easy for the women as I could, while it was going on.

I expected to take the Receiving Matron's place ; but I gave no hint that I expected to do so. I wished to see how the Deputy would manage to obtain the favor from me.

He came in quite early in the morning and said to me, —

" I'm afraid we can't do the kitchen for you to-day.

I don't think the white-wash will dry. It is too damp."

If he sent his men in to white-wash it would be impossible for me to leave, and go to the Receiving Matron's rooms, and oversee the washing. I saw through his plan; but I said, —

" I think I can keep fire enough to dry it. I have made my arrangements to have it done."

" I'll see," he said, and went out.

In a short time the officer who was to oversee the white-washing came in, —

" As it is so damp to-day, the Deputy told me I had better put the men on a job down in the men's workshop; so they won't be in here to-day."

"If the whitening will dry there, why not here? " I asked.

He smiled. " The men have begun there; it won't be best to take them off. I don't think the Deputy would like to have me come in here now."

" I don't think he would," was my knowing reply.

Very soon, Mr. Deputy made his appearance again, and came up to me with a nice, spicy compliment.

"I find it the same here early and late, quiet and clean."

" I'm glad you are pleased with my place."

" Can't you go over to the wash-room, and set the women to work, when they go out from breakfast? And I should like to have you stay there as much as you can this forenoon, to keep order. As it is pea day your women won't have a great deal to do ; and you have got them so well trained they will get on very well without you. You will have no trouble in managing both places."

" O yes, sir ; I will oblige you in that way with pleasure ! "

When they came in to white-wash the kitchen, it rained pouring. The only revenge I took upon the Deputy was to ask him if he thought it would be a good drying day.

XVII.

VISITING DAY.

VISITING day, which came every fourth Wednesday, was a great occasion in the institution.

For two weeks before it was due, the question was continually asked me, —

"Is it next Wednesday, or a week from next Wednesday, that is visiting day? I wonder if my husband will come! I wonder if anybody will come to see me! I want to see the old man so much! I want to hear from the childer so much!"

For a day or two it was my constant care to repress the talk occasioned by the overflowing of their expectations, or fears, so as to get their work done by the women.

The Doctor, when he came to make his visits, passed the kitchen door. That door was made of small panes of ground glass. There was a wooden one inside, to slide over it at night. When he announced his arrival, he had knocked upon one of the panes, with the head of his cane, and broken it. It had been done apparently for mischief; but I thought it was to give the prisoners a glimpse of the blue sky, and the green trees, and the bright flowers that were in front of the prison.

The windows of the kitchen were of the same ground glass, cut into small panes of six by seven. They were made fifty or a hundred years ago, no doubt, with the utilitarian notion of producing greater diligence in the inmates by shutting out all attractive sights which might decoy them from their work. The Matron was taken into the account; her attention must not be drawn from the care of her maidens.

If that were a good rule for the inferior officers and prisoners, why might it not apply with propriety to the Head Matron and Master? The city or state might be saved the large item of expense, in "supporting the institution," of cultivating handsome grounds exclusively for their benefit?

It was a deed of mercy to break that window pane. Many a time when I have seen the lowering brow, or heard the angry remark, I have saved a war of words, perhaps of hands, by sending one of the belligerents to that broken pane to see if the Doctor were on his way to the hospital, or if the bread or meat were coming round.

If I saw the dissatisfaction to be deep-rooted, I gave the command, —

" Stand there and watch a few moments ! "

" That broken pane, on that visiting day, was an outlet for much anxiety. One of the women stood sentinel there all day — sometimes one, sometimes another.

The steam woman, in her anxiety to discover the

approach of her "old man," forgot the care of her boiler, and created quite a scene. She turned the water into it and went to the broken pane to look a moment, forgot it turn it off, and the consequence was an overflow which put out her fire and flooded the floor, — created what McMullins called an "explosion." This she did twice in the forenoon.

The hurry and scurry which was created to relight the fire, and sweep the water down the hatches, diverted the attention of all for a few moments, and passed away the wearisome time of waiting. I pitied the poor old thing as the day wore away, and there was no call for her to go out and see her husband.

"What time is it, if you please, ma'am?" was the continually repeated question when I went near her.

"I don't expect any one to see me," was the remark of the volatile O'Brien.

"Then why do you stand at the window so much to watch?" I asked.

"I want to see who comes to see the others. I want to see if anybody comes in that I know."

Then, the restless thing would mount the window seat. "There goes Johnny, or Charley, or Jimmy, or Dolan." She either saw some of her old associates, with her "two eyes," or through the vision of her imagination. Her suppositions, as to whom they came to see, were as active as her curiosity to see who came.

For the last time the steam woman asked, —

"It is five yet, ma'am?"

I looked at my watch. " Yes, Allen, and five minutes past."

She dropped upon a low table, by which she stood, and burst into tears.

I walked round the kitchen a few times to let her fret spend itself; then I went back, and stood by her side.

" How many children have you, Allen ? "

" Three, ma'am ; two boys and a girl."

" If they were not all right your husband would have come, or sent some one to tell you."

" That's what I'm afraid of, ma'am. The little girl has had a fever. I'm afraid she is worse, or has died, and my husband hates to tell me."

" Perhaps he couldn't leave his work. What does he do ? "

He's a house-builder, ma'am. He's one of the best workmen, ma'am, and they don't like to let him go. He gets three dollars a day, and now he has the whole care of the childer."

" What did you come in here for, Allen ? "

" Shoplifting, ma'am."

" With your husband earning three dollars a day you had no excuse ; that was enough to keep you comfortably."

" So it would, ma'am, if I had been contented. I don't know what made me, — I got a hankering for it. It was eighteen years ago, I was going out to buy me a silk dress, and one of my comrades went with me. I stood looking at a piece of silk, and was going to buy it. She touched my shoulder, 'don't buy that till we look in another store!' When we got out she showed me a piece of silk that she had under her shawl. She got it while I was looking at the other. After that we used to go together."

" Did you ever get caught before ? "

" Yes, ma'am ; I was in here seven years ago."

" And for eighteen years you have followed that wicked life, constantly, and never got caught but twice."

" I never stole from the poor. It was from those that could well afford to spare it. I always took the richest of silks and satins and velvets and linens. Sometimes I had seven or eight hundred dollars' worth at a time."

There was an exhibition of pride in her statement.

The larger the crime, the more honorable, she thought. A strange code of honesty, but a very common one, it would be found, if the practical principles of every person were subjected to analysis.

" But you had no right to the goods ; you paid nothing for them."

" It is the way they do. If a rich customer goes into one of those big stores, they ask him a big price. If a poorer one comes in, and they think he knows what a thing is worth, they don't ask him so much. What is that but stealing ? "

" Their doing wrong does not make it right for you to do wrong. What did you do with what you took ? "

" Sometimes I used it, and sometimes I sold it at

people's doors. I went out West a great many times with a lot."

" What did you intend to do with your money ? "

" Buy a big house, and live in the fashion, when the childer get up."

" Do you think you would enjoy a house bought with money got in that way ? "

" Most of the big houses are bought with money got in that way. I know many a person as has carried on the business for years, and got rich by it."

" The business of shoplifting ! then the crime has become dignified into a business." Rather a liberal translation of the example set, I thought.

" Did your husband know what you were doing ? "

" Yes, ma'am."

" Did he approve of it ? "

" No, ma'am ; he always warned me, and sometimes forbid me. But as soon as he was off to his work, I would shift my clothes and go out. I hurried back, and got them shifted again before he came home ; and he wouldn't know it till I had got a great many pieces."

" Does he turn against you now ? "

" O no ! He is a good man ; and he cried when I came here, — for me and the poor childer. He pitied me, and told me how hard it would be on me, seein' I was never used to it."

Crazy Manhattan came up just in time to hear the last sentence.

" An' sure it is hard on her ! I've known her out-

11

side, and she's not bein' used to lift her finger to work."

" She had better have been, than to have been lifting her finger to take other people's goods."

" Give me a slice of bread, ma'am, an' you please! I've been ironing in the wash-room, and I've done your own things beautifully. Don't tell the Deputy!" she said, as she slipped it under her apron and ran away.

" I knew her a little outside," said the steam woman ; " but she was nothing but a house thief!"

Well, well! the fashions of society obtain among thieves as well as the principles. A shop lifter ranks in a higher grade than a house thief.

I talked with Allen some time, and tried to show her that whatever others might do was no excuse for her in wrong doing. At last she admitted it ; but wound up by saying, —

"Ise got such an itching in my fingers for it, I couldn't help taking the things."

The patience which is required to inculcate right principles, where wrong ones have been practiced for half a century, is incalculable. But it does not come in comparison with that which is exercised towards us by the long-suffering Father of our spirits.

XVIII.

CALLAHAN AGAIN.

I stood by the mush-boiler, one morning, calculating the probabilities of having that delicacy well
cooked by eleven o'clock, so that a second edition
might be issued before night, when I heard the cry
out in the prison, —

"Callahan is coming! Callahan is coming! they've
had an awful row at the shop!"

I had some idea of what a row with Callahan
meant. I had been told that she had snatched the
Master's wig from his head, torn it in bits, and scattered it to the winds; that she had pulled the
Deputy's watch from his pocket, and stamped it beneath her feet; that she had ripped their coats open
with her fingers, and scratched their faces like a cat.
I had heard that she gloried in being the worst
tempered woman in the shop, in being stronger than
a man, and bragged that it took two to confine her.
To me she had always been respectful and obedient,
even when in solitary.

Once, when I saw her speak while marching into
prison, I "admonished" her.

"Callahan, you know it is against the rules to talk
when you are coming in; you won't do it again?"

" No, ma'am ; but Callahan isn't my name, now ; that was my first husband's name. It is Good-enough, now. Please call me Goodenough !"

" I will call you so; and I hope you will be good enough when you are under my care."

" I will be good when I am under your care."

That was all the experience I had had in reprov-ing, or punishing, Callahan when she had offended in my presence. And that was the only offense she had committed.

The noise of voices grew loud in the yard. O'Brien came running up to me, —

" Please come out here, ma'am. They have had an awful time with Callahan, I know by the way she swears ; but she will mind you if you speak to her. She behaves well enough if she is only treated half decent."

I went to the door. Callahan was coming up the walk between two officers, raving frightfully, shout-ing and swearing. When she came into the entry she smashed her hand through every pane of glass that she could reach, gashing her arms and spatter-ing the blood on the floor and walls.

As soon as I could get her attention, which it took me some time to do, she was so excited, I spoke to her, —

" Callahan, stop! haven't you promised to be a good woman when you are with me ? "

She looked at me, lowered her voice, but kept on with her talk. In a few moments I spoke again, —

" Callahan, stop !"

She turned to me, and answered, but pleasantly, —

" Can't the Deputy take care of me?"

" Certainly! but you ought to have respect enough to my feelings to talk decently where I am."

" I have cut my hands awfully; " and she held out her arm towards me.

" Yes, you have. Shall I bind it up for you?"

I sent for bandages and water, and bound up her hands and arms. She washed the blood-stains from her clothes, and made herself tidy.

" That will do, Callahan! We want to lock you in now."

She looked at the key which I held in my hand.

" I am ready; lock me up."

The key was turned, and Callahan was in solitary again.

Not long afterwards, when all was quiet, I passed her door. She called to me, —

" Look here!"

" Well, Callahan."

" I'm sorry I talked so bad before you; but I was so mad I didn't know what I said. I've got no spite against you."

" I am sorry you have against any one."

" O that she-d—l in the shop! I'd send her into eternity if I could get hold of her!"

" Stop, Callahan! will you be gentle and patient while you are here with me?"

" Yes, for you I will. But look here! my arm pains me, and it's swelled awfully! I'm afraid there's glass in it."

"I think you can see the Doctor if you wish. I think he had better see it. I'll go ask the Deputy to send him in."

"Thank you; I wish you would. I'm afraid there's glass in it, and it will be awful sore if it stays there."

I whistled for the Deputy, told him what Callahan said, and he sent the Doctor in.

When she was first locked in he had told me not to open her cell unless he were present. He was a new Deputy who had come into office that day, and evidently felt the responsibility that was attached to his office, and the consequence it gave him.

"You will come round when it is time to give her food?"

"Yes."

I thought he was afraid of her violence; but I had no apprehension on that score, so when the Doctor came, not thinking of the order, I opened the cell as I had always done under the other Deputy. I had occasion to think, afterwards, that he did not wish her to tell her own story, unless it was in his presence; or intended to prevent her altogether.

The front door of the kitchen stood open, and the Doctor came in that way without seeing any of the officers.

"What is the matter here?" he asked in his jolly way; "who is cut to pieces?"

"Callahan has cut herself," I answered, as I went to get the key to open her cell.

" How did she do it ? "

" She got angry and struck her hand through the window."

" Is that the way you do when you get angry ? "

" Did you come here to treat me ? "

" Women are a great deal alike, are they not ? "

" You make an assertion, and ask me to confirm it."

" Isn't it so ? "

" As much alike as different men, if you are really interested to know my opinion."

" How about the other ? "

" You wish to understand my disposition, do you ? I am happy to gratify you on that point so far as my knowledge goes. There is method in my madness. I usually consider the matter awhile, or sulk ; then, make a thorough application of the dictionary to the offending party. Look out for yourself or you may get a blow sometime from Webster's Unabridged."

I had opened the black cell door.

" What are you in here again for so soon, Callahan ? Let me see your arm."

She reached out her arm, and the Doctor took off the bandages.

" I'll tell you the truth, Doctor."

" Tell away."

" I called to little red-headed Jones, — you know that little dumpy thing that fetches the work for us, — I called to Jones to fetch me some work. She was talking to that little fire-brand of a Harlan that takes care of the engine in the work-room. Well, you see, she felt so nice to be taken notice of by Harlan, that she wouldn't mind when I spoke. She pretended not to hear. I called louder, 'Jones, fetch me some work.' Jones was mad then, and said, 'I'll fetch it when I please.' Then I told her to fetch me some work now, and do her talking afterwards: 'That's what you're here for,' I said. Harlan was mad, and went straight out into the men's shop and reported me. The Master and the Deputy came right in, and made towards me. I was mad; for if anybody was reported it ought to be Harlan and Jones, for it is against the rules for them to be talking together; but 'twasn't against the rules for me to ask for work. When I saw the Master and the Deputy coming straight to me, to lock me up, I pulled up a chair to knock him down, I was so mad to think I was going to be locked up for nothing, and Jones to be let go when she had been breaking the rules. And Harlan to report me, when he helped her break 'em. The little spit-fire!"

"Why didn't you wait and see if you were going to be locked up, and tell the Master how it was, before you took up a chair to strike him down?" I asked.

"She's green, Doctor! Tell him! he wouldn't let me tell him anything! Many's the time I've been locked up and didn't know what 'twas for. Look here, wouldn't it make you mad to be locked up when you wasn't to blame? Look here, do you blame me for being mad?"

I could not say yes, and tell the truth. There is not a human heart but what would resent such injustice. There are but few who would not resist it if they could. I could not say no, because it might be construed into encouraging insubordination. I did not feel it incumbent on me to think the Master in the right because he was the Master, and she the convict. I deliberately committed the vulgarity of listening to a convict's story; but did not think it necessary to tell her my thoughts.

"Callahan, you mustn't ask me such questions. I am sorry for you, and will make you as comfortable as I can."

The doctor put some compresses on her arm, wet them with water, and ordered her some to drink.

"Some water for Callahan to drink! Quick! The doctor has ordered it!" I echoed. I thought I heard an officer's step at the farther end of the prison, and it was a legitimate supposition that if it were the new Deputy, who was coming, she would get no such favor. Unless she got the water and drank it before he came, she would not get it at all.

It had been whispered to me that the Master had thrown Callahan on the floor in his anger, when she caught up the chair, and put his foot on her neck. I saw a mark of dirt on the lower part of her cheek and neck. I looked closely at it. The skin was grazed as though a boot-heel had been ground against it.

"Callahan, what is that dirt on your cheek and neck?" I asked.

She put up her hand and passed it across her face and neck at the place where I saw the dirt. She knew exactly where to find the mark of which I spoke. The boot had evidently been there.

"He did hurt me some," she said.

"Who?" I asked.

"The Master, he put his foot on me."

"On your cheek and neck?"

"Yes, ma'am."

"What for?"

"To hold me down."

"Let me see."

I examined the flesh; it was a little discolored as though it had been bruised. It was evident that the tale that had been told me was true. Was it necessary for that man — or the monster — in taking the chair away from that woman, with two men to help him, to throw her upon the floor, and place his foot on her neck?

"He was pretty well seas over. He's always savage when he is. I knew he'd just had a horn when I saw him coming, and that's one thing made me mad. Look here; folks are sent down here for getting drunk. Do you think it'll ever cure 'em to put a drunkard over 'em?"

I did not make Callahan any reply; but I thought of the old proverb, "It takes a rogue to catch a rogue;" but whether a rogue may be advantageously set to cure one, is another question, and one upon which a great deal of discussion might be spent, before popular judgment would decide it in the affirmative.

Callahan had just finished washing the dirt from her face when the Deputy made his appearance.

" I gave the order that Callahan's cell should not be opened unless I was here."

" The doctor came, I supposed you sent him, and opened the cell door as I always do for him."

" What way did he come in ? "

" Through the front door of the kitchen, as he often does."

I was not sorry for the mistake.

That evening Mrs. Hardhack told me they were determined to break Callahan's temper. They had got her pretty well under; but it was not quite broken.

Her constitution was in a fair way to be broken, her temper might share the same fate. If to teach her to control her temper were what was meant, a very unfit method was adopted to effect the purpose.

How can one person teach another to control his temper when he is ignorant of the way, and does not practice the government of his own?

When I was left alone in the prison, I sat down before Callahan's cell door. I thought over the object of punishment. Is it intended to deter the vicious from continuing in crime ? That is the apparent object. Then, ought it not to be adapted to the crime, and administered by those who are free from the same faults? Instead of that, it was left, in this instance, an almost irresponsible power, in the hands of ignorance and cruelty, and if report were not mistaken, of kindred sin.

I thought, some mother's heart is aching for you, poor Callahan ; such treatment as you receive here, will never lead you to make it ache the less. Injustice and severity will never soften your heart, or enlighten your understanding. God pity you, and interpose in your behalf!

" What are you thinking of? " asked Callahan.

" How did you know that I was thinking ? "

" I looked through the key-hole, and saw you looking straight to the floor, biting your nails."

" I was thinking of you, Callahan."

" You was thinking what a wicked wretch I am ? "

" I wish you might become better, and never come in this place again. It is a great deal of suffering for so little comfort as you can take in sin. Won't you try to do better, Callahan ? "

" I can't in here. They are just as bad as I am that put me in here, and they'll never make me any better."

There was the injustice for which she had suffered rankling in her heart.

" It is more what we do ourselves than what others do to us which makes us happy or unhappy."

" It's what they've done to me that makes me unhappy, and if ever I catch them —— outside, I'll pay 'em back, — I will, if I go to h—l for it ! "

" Callahan, Callahan, be patient and gentle! Don't think of any wicked things to do outside, but think how to behave so that you can stay there. Remember it was for your own deeds that you came in here. If you hadn't been in here, they couldn't have put you in the black cell. Be gentle and patient while you are here, now that it can't be helped, and never come again."

"For you, I will; and I'll try not to go in the ways that bring me here. But if I should meet them, I know I should forget it all. I should think about it, and it would make me so mad. If I was out of the right way, and got in here, the Master had no right to lock me up here for what I did not do."

I had no justification of that proceeding to offer, so I said nothing more.

"Will you please give me a drink of water?" asked Callahan in a moment.

"Callahan, you know that I cannot! Why do you hurt my feelings by asking me?"

"You have the keys, — you could give it to me, and the Deputy would never know it. If you knew how dry I am you would."

"I cannot, Callahan. When I go out of here I can tell those who make the rules, how hard it is to go so long without drinking, and how tiresome it is to lie, and sit, and stand on the stones, and perhaps they will change them; but I cannot disobey."

"O dear!" she sighed, and began to sing. Every sound went through my heart like the stab of a sharp knife. If that were my child! was the agonizing thought. What keeps my children from such a

fate? The loving care of Him who holds the hearts
of all in His hand. I could have gone prostrate on
the cold stones to thank Him that He had saved
them from such a fate, and me from such an agony
of sorrow. How can I show my gratitude? By trying to make less hard the hapless lot of the unfor-
tunates around me, and teaching them in the principles that lead to better practices.

My tears almost choked my utterance as I called
to her, "Callahan, stop that singing unless you mean
to break my heart!"

O'Brien had been standing on the steps that led
to the kitchen, only a few feet from me. She came
along and sat down on a low stool at my feet.

"How different you are to what I thought you
was when you came in here. You stepped round so
square and independent, I thought we had got a
hard mistress."

"Look here!" said Callahan, "it does me good
to speak to you sometimes. It is easier to be patient,
and the time don't seem so long. Look here! Do
you love Hardhack?"

"I know very little about her."

"I heard her in the kitchen scolding awhile ago,
and you took it as cool as could be. If I'd been
you I'd put her out. She has no right to come in
your place and give orders. It sets me crazy to hear
her."

"If I could not keep my own temper when I am
annoyed, how could I teach you to keep yours?"

"That's it," said O'Brien. "Hardhack gets mad in the shop, and scolds us, and we scold back; and then we get punished. I wish there was somebody to report her, too."

"Girls, did you ever hear of One who said, 'Love your enemies, bless them that curse you'?"

"Yes; but I never saw anybody do it," said O'Brien.

"Did you ever try to do it, Callahan?"

"No! I always thought 'twas all moonshine. It'll do to preach about."

"It will do to practice, too. Suppose you try it towards Mrs. Hardhack, and see how much happier you will feel."

"Ha! ha! ha!" resounded through the prison in continuous echoes.

"It has done me good to laugh. I don't feel half so mad with her as I did."

"O'Brien, I came very near sending you to the shop to-day, when you scolded Allen so hard. Be careful or you will change your mistress before you know it. You keep me in constant anxiety lest the Deputy, or some of the other Matrons should come in and hear you. In that case it would be beyond my power to help you."

"If you do send me to the shop you will have me home again in less than twenty-four hours, one of your bread-and-water boarders."

She understood how to meet that threat.

"I don't know but Hardhack will get me into sol-

itary as it is. When she came through the kitchen
this noon, she saw me eating a piece of fish with my
bread, — we'd been stripping it off for the hash, and
I took a piece. She asked me who gave me liberty
to eat fish. I told her, nobody. She asked me how
I dared to eat that fish without permission. I should
have made her a saucy answer only I knew it would
make you feel bad, so I didn't say anything."

" I am glad you had so much thought, and exercised so much self-control."

" I wasn't afraid of Hardhack."

" I am glad you had so much regard for me. It
gives me a great deal of pleasure to know of your
good behavior. Don't you feel better, yourself, for
doing what is right?"

" Yes, ma'am; I do! and when you tell me I do
right, it makes me feel quite like a woman again ; as
though I was somebody."

Self-respect goes a long way towards creating good
behavior, and commendation given, where it is deserved, produces that effect. I watched for a chance
to praise them when they did well, and bestowed the
approval wherever I could find the opportunity.

There was no lack of discrimination on their part.
They were aware when they committed intentional
wrong, and, as a rule, acknowledged it when rebuked
in a kind spirit. With the same understanding they
appreciated the praise when it was deserved. Gratitude was aroused when it was given, and the satisfaction they enjoyed was an incentive to strive to
obtain more.

I had constant proof that the exercise of kindness was far more effectual in getting my work done than that of stern authority.

That afternoon I had wished O'Brien to take more pains with her scrubbing, and had said to her, —

"Your floor looks red and nice," — the kitchen floor was of brick, — "but do you notice that soiled strip in that corner, under the table? A dingy border spoils all the effect of your labor."

"Yes, ma'am. I saw it when I was scrubbing; but I was so tired, and my shoulder ached so bad that I didn't touch it."

"I am sorry your shoulder aches, and I know you are tired; but I like to see the place look nice."

"I know you do; I'll go right now and take it away."

Kindness begets kindness. There are few human beings so totally depraved, desperately wicked as some may be, who cannot be aroused into appreciation of kind treatment. I have never met with one who could not. So harshness in a superior begets harshness in an inferior; and constant fault-finding either arouses anger from its injustice, or paralyzes all effort to do well.

As are the manners of those who lead, so are the manners of those who follow. As a matter of policy, to restrain crime without regard to the teaching of religion, those who have charge of convicts should be gentle and humane.

12

XIX.

DISCOMFORTS, AND THE END.

A VERY few days after I entered the institution, I gave up looking for any consideration from any one but the Deputy.

It was a rule of the place to shift every labor, when it could be effected, by the one to whom it belonged, upon some other person. That is, in the female department. The example set by the Head Matron was considered worthy of imitation, and copied with an accuracy deserved by a better one.

To impose upon an officer, ignorant of the ways of the place, was a favorite entertainment of some of the others.

They commenced to hand me along from one to another when I wished for things to use, or for information, giving me a long chase to find it; but a short time, only, was required to extinguish that entertainment. I refused to take orders or information from any one but the Deputy.

My inquiries of him, and statements of what I had been told, exposed them. They got reproof instead of entertainment, which, of course, created resentment that vented itself in a thousand of those little annoying inventions in which unamiable women are so ingenious.

The reprisals Mrs. Hardhack made did not always redound to my inconvenience alone, — my women came in for a share in the retaliation. A new Receiving Matron was told to take no trouble about the dresses of my women in the kitchen, — it was no matter how they looked. The shorter she kept them, the better the Master would like it. The less they had to wear the more money would be saved to the institution. In consequence, dresses sufficient to make them decent were withheld.

I made a statement of some of these things to the Deputy. He said, —

"The Matrons have been in the habit of settling those small matters among themselves."

"So we might if either of us had the authority to dictate. If Mrs. Hardhack has the authority to control, and gives the order that my women are to go dirty and ragged, as you see them, I appeal to you. Just look at them as you see them now. Those dresses are all they have, and I can get no better without an order from you."

He looked at them. The angry color flashed into his face, and his teeth were set together. In about two hours tidy dresses were sent in to my women.

I went on, —

"If she has no authority, but is meddling to make mischief, will you please see that she does it no longer. I know it is not the Deputy's business to

be settling these little disagreements among the
Matrons; but I have no one else to go to. We have
no one to regulate these matters for us but you. You
call them small matters; so they may be to one who
looks on; but our life, every day, is made up of
them. And if you take them home, and make them
your own, you will not think them so very small.
Neither you nor I would consider it a small matter to
go dirty and ragged. Would you allow one of your
male officers to keep the men who are under another
officer dirty and ragged, out of sheer malice, or for
any reason?"

"They could not do it, — I should not allow it."

"And you are there to see it, and have the authority to prevent it. And as you have undertaken to
do the duty of the Head Officer on this side, I see
no other way but to appeal to you in these cases of
ours. I have no authority to prevent the mischievous
interference of Mrs. Hardhack; and to aggravate,
in return, I cannot. She has the advantage of me
in the disposition and ability to do so. She has
ample opportunity to meddle with the affairs of the
other Matrons, because they are sent to her for instruction; and also to give her interpretation of the
Rules. Mrs. Hardhack is not so much to blame for
what she does. She is only following the bent of her
own disposition, as the opportunity to do so is given
her. The Head Matron comes to me, and says, —
' Control your own place. Mrs. Hardhack has
nothing to do with it. If she makes trouble with

another Matron, she shall surely be discharged. She has been discharged three times, and begged herself back ; but if we say to her, go again, she will surely go.' Then she goes to Mrs. Hardhack, and says, — ' You go over to the wash-room and tell the Receiving Matron about her place. You know all about the Rules and things better than I do. I don't know what I should do without you.' That pleases Mrs. Hardhack, and she meddles with everything, and makes trouble all around."

" I will do all I can to help you."

" I know ; but I am tired. The care is altogether too much, and the mismanagement of the place makes it intolerable. Explain to the Receiving Matron, if you please, that she is under obligation to wash and mend the clothes of my women the same that she does the others, and give them out another dress when one fails."

" I will do that."

That night I was speaking of the severe labor required of the officers in the institution to Mrs. Hardhack. She turned to me, and said roughly, — " I find it easy enough."

It was just the right moment for me to tell her why she found it so much easier than the rest of us.

" You may well find it so, in comparison with the rest of us. You have an hour more of rest in the morning than I, and an hour more at night, making nine hours of rest from labor in the twenty-four, instead of the seven that I have. During those nine hours you are entirely free from care, and sleep in a quiet room in the house. During the fifteen that you are on duty you have the entire help of the only Relief Matron in the institution, which ought to be divided among us all, so that you can go out when you please."

"Perhaps, when you have been in the institution as long as I, you will get as many favors."

"I could not take them, if I got them by robbery. I could not enjoy my liberty if the work which belonged to me were imposed upon another, making her burden double, for me to have it."

A smart rap was all the woman could feel. I really grew in her esteem by cutting her up with my sharpness, and she attempted to ingratiate herself into my favor. I will relate how, and how I discovered it.

The next night I was called to lock a woman in solitary. She walked into her cell in silence, and I as silently turned the key upon her. I did not ask the Deputy why she was put there. She was brought up from the shop, and I supposed some miserable tale was appended to her incarceration which I did not care to know.

The next morning, when I went to give her bread and water, she asked me, —

"Do you know what I am in here for?"

"No; I haven't heard them say."

"It was for mocking you. I know it was wrong; but the others did it, and I did it too, and I got caught."

" Who caught you ? "

" Mrs. Hardhack. I know it was wrong, I was foolish, but I'll never do it again. The others did it, and so I did it, too."

" And you hadn't courage to do right when others were doing wrong. You are a brave girl! Do you know that there must be order kept in this place, and that there must be rules in order to keep order, and that you must treat those who have the rules in charge with respect ? "

" Yes, ma'am ; and I never will do it again. Will you get me out ? "

" I'll try ; but you must always treat me with respect, and all of the other officers in the same way. I shall never intercede for you again."

" I will never give you any reason to."

When the Deputy came round I asked, —

" Is Mary Muran in solitary for mimicking me ? "

He said, " Yes."

" Was it for the second offense ? Had she been admonished once ? "

" She knew better."

" Your Rules and Regulations make no conditions that they know better. They shall be admonished once, and, for the second offense punished."

" They wouldn't do exactly the same thing twice, perhaps ; but they would do something as near like it as they could."

" We have no help for that, if we obey the Rules."

" We should be constantly admonishing."

"Wouldn't that be better than constantly punishing? Isn't it better to err on the side of mercy than on that of severity? It seems to me a very severe punishment to put upon a girl for so slight an offense. I think I could have administered a rebuke that would have prevented her repeating it towards me. It really makes me very unhappy to think she is locked up there for a disrespect shown me."

"If you are satisfied with the punishment she has had, you can let her out."

"Indeed I am!"

If she had been one of my women perhaps I should not have reminded the Deputy that he had transcended his orders. Mary Muran was a shop woman. When she was released from her solitary confinement she would return to the shop. Mrs. Hardhack would call him to account for letting her off with so slight a punishment. I gave him an answer for her.

I went directly to the girl's cell.

"You can go, Mary, and I hope you will never do so mean and foolish a thing as to mimic a Matron again."

"I never will, and I shall always remember this kindness in you."

I never knew her to require reproof again, while I was in the institution. It was like the experience I had with every other prisoner. There are, undoubtedly, those who return kindness with ingratitude, but I never saw the kindness fail to produce good behavior while there.

The long day's work, the night vigils, and the damp, noisome air of the prison, were telling upon my health. I was getting an intermittent pulse; chills and fainting every other morning.

I asked the Housekeeper to let me have a cup of tea at half past six. Unless I took it then, I was obliged to wait another hour, because I must attend to giving out the breakfast of the prisoners. In doing that duty I was made a three hours and a half watch before I had anything to eat in the morning. She had given her permission for me to have it; and I had availed myself of the privilege.

One morning after setting my women about the work I wished to have done, while I was gone, I went in to breakfast.

Supervisor arose about that time, and made the important discovery, to her, that the fire had gone out in her furnace, and her parlor was cold. This was in May, consequently the weather was not very inclement.

Her parlor was directly over the prisoners' kitchen; her front door over the kitchen door. The steps that led up to her apartments went past our windows. She often ran down these steps, and looked in the window to give an order about the furnace. This morning she did so, and, not seeing me, inquired where I was.

" Gone in to breakfast," was the reply.

Annie O'Brien, who had charge of the furnace, brought me the order as soon as I went in.

" Shall I have time to do it ? " she asked.

"No; it wants but eight minutes of breakfast time. It will take all of that time to " dish up " your mush, and get your coffee ready. It will take half an hour to clear the furnace and light the fire. I am sorry ; but you will be obliged to wait till after breakfast."

Supervisor grew impatient, and the more impatient she was the colder she grew. Her comfort was the first thing to be attended to in that institution. The prisoners might go without their breakfast, — the Matrons might faint away for want of food, — it was only paying her proper respect to light her fire, as soon as the order was given.

I was in her power, she could retaliate upon me.

That evening I met her in the officers' dining-room, and asked her if she wished me to keep a three hours and a half watch before breakfast. She replied, —

" It has been done thirty-three years."

" Great changes have taken place in the world during the last thirty-three years, and many more might be effected with advantage," I remarked.

" I don't see how you can find time to go to breakfast at that hour."

" I should not find time at any hour unless I took it."

" That is so; but they were dishing out when I went down. You ought to be there when they are dishing out."

"I suppose so; but I have an order to be in the prison a large part of the time, at all three of the meals, when they are dishing out, and they are obliged to do it without my oversight." Doing your duty, I would have liked to have added.

"Most of the officers like to go to table with the others for company."

"I did not come here for society. In wishing to breakfast earlier, I was not consulting my taste, but trying to take care of my health. Unless I am made somewhat comfortable, I shall break down, and be obliged to leave."

"Comfortable!" she echoed. I was not surprised that the word sounded so strangely to her, connected with any other person than herself.

Discipline had become a mania, and it was applied as severely to the officers as the prisoners, so far as it was in her power to effect it.

The whole study, it appeared to me, was to keep them on duty all day, without relaxation ; and they were cut off from every means of enjoyment which was not connected with their care.

There was a common sitting-room where the male officers and Matrons sat and talked together, when they were not on duty, when I went there ; but that was taken away, and made into a bed-room, so that there was no place for them to meet except in their own bed-rooms, the halls, or on the grounds.

If human ingenuity were to set itself to work to invent a position of unmitigated discomfort, that

prison life would give some excellent hints. The
heads of the establishment were certainly very keen
in discovering ways to circumscribe the comforts of
its inmates.

I made a statement of my circumstances to Supervisor; not with any expectation of obtaining any
consideration, but merely to place my view of things
before her.

"You cannot wonder that I do not consider that
I am made comfortable when you think of my seventeen hours of labor in the day, to which is added the
care of the prison, nights."

"The care of the prison, nights!" she echoed, and
turned up her nose in disdain.

I did not explain; but reminded her that the
Housekeeper had two hours and a half more rest in
the morning than I.

"I am glad she can have it; and it would be only
kind to give me my tea a little earlier, as I cannot
have it."

"She has to be up nights frequently."

"No oftener than I, and not so late. I lock her
women up after she dismisses them from her
kitchen."

"I shall lose a good Housekeeper if you have your
breakfast before the rest. She won't stay if she is
obliged to get it."

"She told me she was willing I should have it."

"She is unwilling now."

I readily saw why she had become unwilling. She

herself had made up her mind that it was not to be given me, because I delayed the kindling of her fire, and she had made the Housekeeper unwilling.

" You had better keep her. It is doubtful if I could remain with that favor. It is with great difficulty that I get through the day now, with the help of a tonic that the Doctor has given me."

I sent in my resignation the next morning. I told the Master that I would stay till he could find some one to take my place.

As I was no longer an officer on duty, merely a temporary supply of help, I took the liberty to go back to bed, after I had called the women out, to get an additional hour or two of sleep. I found that it helped me wonderfully in getting through the day.

When the Deputy came round, I reported myself.

" You did not do your duty ! " was his curt reply.

" I am not on duty and I shall do it every morning that I stay here to oblige you. If I were the only one in the institution who does not do her duty, it would be well to single me out for reproof. Indeed I am not sure that I am not doing my duty — to myself. If the women in the officers' kitchen can work two hours and a half in the morning without a mistress, so that the Housekeeper can get her rest, why may not the women in the prisoners' kitchen do the same thing, so that their Matron may get rest ? "

The Deputy smiled at my reasoning. " I cannot discipline you ; you are not one of the officers of the institution now. I get up nearly as early as you do."

" I hope you enjoy it."

"I cannot say that I exactly enjoy it; but my duty calls me, and I do it."

" You are a strong, healthy man, and can bear a great deal of care. But you do not have as much as I. You have your rest through the night without it. You have your watchman in prison, and go to your bed in the house. That prison is no place for a woman to sleep in, and the care of it is no work for a woman, who works all day,—and for no one else who is obliged to be on duty through the day."

" It is hardly fit work for a woman to sleep in a prison, and take care of it nights."

" Aside from its fitness I cannot do it for want of strength. I hope you will find some one to take my place very soon. I saw two or three advertisements in last night's paper for such a place."

The next morning, I fainted in attempting to rise, and was obliged to go down in my night-dress and shawls to call the women out.

I should have told the Master that day that I could rise no longer to call the women out, only that I heard that Mrs. Hardhack wished to go out that night, to return at seven the next morning. If I refused to get up, she would be obliged to stay at home to do that duty.

I thought I would heap one coal of kindness on her head, so I told her I would try to get through with it one more morning. She accepted the favor; but it was like casting pearls before swine — she did not thank me.

As soon as she returned the next morning, I wrote the Master a note, saying I could rise no longer to call the women out, and I hoped he would find some one to relieve me of all duty as soon as possible.

He took no notice of my note till afternoon; then I heard him, in his measured tread, stalking along the prison floor. The dinner was out of the way; nearly all of the work attended to for the day. The time I had spent from morning till afternoon was so much gained for which he did not pay.

"You are not willing to get up and unlock any longer in the morning, you say?"

"I cannot, sir; I am too ill."

"Then we don't want you here any longer," was the gentlemanly response.

"I am happy to be relieved of my duties here."

"You may go now, the sooner the better," was his gentle reply.

"Yes, sir; I will leave directly."

I called my maid, packed my trunk, and made all haste to depart. I made my adieus as brief as possible. My women, with one exception, were crying and lamenting my departure, and I truly regretted to leave the poor wretches in such merciless care.

"I shall spend the rest of my time in solitary," said O'Brien.

"I shall get locked up the first thing," said Lissett.

"I shall try to get into the shop," said Allen. "I never can stand it here after ye."

"My heart is as black after ye as that stove," sobbed McMullins.

It was many a day and night, after I went out from that prison, before the sights and sounds that I saw and heard there left my mental sight and hearing.

I thought as I went away, I will go from door to door through this broad Commonwealth, state what I have learned of woman's condition in prison, and beseech every other woman to help open the doors of her ignorance, and degradation, to the light of the knowledge which will lead to reformation.

Every one who has the cause of humanity at heart will echo the cry, — open the doors of our prisons, as the doors of other public institutions are thrown open, so that those who support may have an opportunity to inspect them.

It is the right of every tax-payer to know what is done within our prison walls at all times. It is the duty of every Christian man to make himself acquainted with the moral bearing of the discipline which obtains within them.

It is the duty of every religious woman to see that her fellow woman is not trampled down in degradation and vice, lower than her own sins would carry her, by the heel of her master in discipline.

Let the prison doors be opened, and the inside of them exposed to the view of all. Knowledge awakens interest, and interest leads to action.

If the people of this land could be roused to examine the subject, our prisons would soon be managed upon principles which would tend to the elevation of the wretched beings who now come out of them more degraded and hardened in the commission of crime than they go in.

God grant that the day filled with such blessing for the poor convict, be not far distant !

www.ingramcontent.com/pod-product-compliance
Lightning Source LLC
Chambersburg PA
CBHW030830020726
47499CB00006B/2137